Strangers on a Train

Nancy Drew DIARIES™

Strangers on a Train

#2

CAROLYN KEENE

Aladdin
NEW YORK LONDON TORONTO SYDNEY NEW DELHI

ALADDIN

An imprint of Simon & Schuster Children's Publishing Division

1230 Avenue of the Americas, New York, NY 10020

First Aladdin paperback edition February 2013

Copyright © 2013 by Simon & Schuster

All rights reserved, including the right of reproduction in whole or in part in any form.

ALADDIN is a trademark of Simon & Schuster, Inc., and related logo is a registered trademark of Simon & Schuster, Inc.

NANCY DREW, NANCY DREW DIARIES, and related logo are trademarks of Simon & Schuster, Inc.

Also available in an Aladdin hardcover edition.

For information about special discounts for bulk purchases, please contact Simon & Schuster Special Sales at 1-866-506-1949 or business@simonandschuster.com.

The Simon & Schuster Speakers Bureau can bring authors to your live event. For more information or to book an event contact the Simon & Schuster Speakers Bureau at 1-866-248-3049 or visit our website at www.simonspeakers.com.

Designed by Karina Granda

The text of this book was set in Adobe Caslon Pro.

Manufactured in the United States of America 1214 OFF

6 8 10 9 7 5

Library of Congress Control Number 2012949339

ISBN 978-1-4169-9073-4 (pbk)

ISBN 978-1-4424-6611-1 (hc)

ISBN 978-1-4424-6571-8 (eBook)

Contents

HOW DID IT HAPPEN?

How did someone ever figure out I was a detective, working undercover?

Bess, George, and I have been posing as contest-winning passengers aboard the *Arctic Star*, and I thought I had pretty much solved the mystery on this amazing cruise ship.

But now it seems as though *I'm* being targeted. My luggage and laundry have been ransacked, and when we were traveling to Denali, I was almost cut to shreds by jagged glass.

I always cover my every move. . . .

Don't I?

CHAPTER ONE

Going Ashore

"NANCY! DOWN HERE!"

I hurried down the last few steps to the landing and saw Becca Wright waving as she rushed up the next set of steps toward me. The cruise ship's atrium stairwell was deserted except for the two of us, just as she'd predicted. Almost everyone aboard the *Arctic Star* was gathered along the open-air decks watching the view as the ship chugged into the picturesque port of Skagway, Alaska.

"I don't have much time," I told Becca. "Alan thinks I'm in the ladies' room. He wants to get a photo of all of us at the rail when we dock."

"I don't have much time either." Becca checked her watch. As the *Arctic Star*'s assistant cruise director, she was always busy. "I'm supposed to be getting ready for disembarkation right now. But I just found out something I thought you'd want to know right away. The police caught the robber!"

I gasped, flashing back to the events of the day before yesterday. While the ship was docked in a town called Ketchikan, someone had robbed the shipboard jewelry store.

"Really, they caught someone already? That's amazing!" I exclaimed. "Who was it?"

"A guy named Troy Anderson," Becca replied, leaning down to pluck a stray bit of lint off the carpet. "I guess he's well known to the local authorities as a petty thief and general troublemaker type. They caught him over in Juneau trying to fence the stuff he stole."

I blinked, taking that in. It wasn't exactly the answer I'd been expecting. "So he wasn't a passenger or crew member on the *Arctic Star*?"

Becca raked a hand through her dark curls. "Nope.

Which is weird, right? I have no idea how he got onboard." She smiled weakly. "Maybe it's a good thing you're still here, Nancy. I hope you're in the mood for another mystery?"

The *Arctic Star* was the flagship of the brand-new Superstar Cruises, and this was its maiden voyage. However, things had gone wrong from the start. *Before* the start, actually. That was why Becca had called me. We'd known each other for years, and she knew I liked nothing better than investigating a tough mystery. She'd called me in—along with my two best friends, Bess Marvin and George Fayne—because she was worried that someone was trying to sabotage the new ship.

And she'd been right. Just a few days into the cruise, I'd nabbed the saboteurs, Vince and Lacey. They were working for a rival cruise line, trying to put Superstar out of business.

Then the jewelry store robbery happened—*after* Vince and Lacey were in custody. And I'd realized that maybe the mystery wasn't over after all.

"Do you think this Anderson guy had an accomplice on the ship?" I asked. "If so, maybe that person was also responsible for some of the other stuff that's been going wrong."

Becca bit her lip, looking anxious. "I hope not. Because I was really hoping all the trouble would be over after you busted Vince and Lacey."

I knew what she meant. I'd been trying to convince myself that the case was solved. That a few dangling loose ends didn't matter. That those loose ends were just red herrings, easily explained by bad luck, coincidence, whatever.

What kind of loose ends? Well, for instance, there was the threatening note I'd found in my suitcase the first day onboard. Vince and Lacey claimed to know nothing about that. They also denied being involved in most of the problems that had happened before the ship set sail. And they claimed to know nothing about the fake moose antler from the mini-golf course that had missed crushing me by inches. They also seemed clueless about the angry argument I'd overheard from the ship's kitchen that had ended in what sounded like a threat: *Drop it, John! Or I'll make sure you never make it to Anchorage.* And they insisted that neither of them was the person who'd pushed me off a raised walkway in Ketchikan, sending me tumbling twenty feet down into icy water.

I shivered, thinking back over the list. It didn't take an expert detective to realize that the most serious of those incidents seemed to be directed at yours truly.

"We have to accept that the case might not be over quite yet," I told Becca. "If the robber does have an accomplice on this ship, he or she might still try to cause more trouble. We'll have to keep our eyes open for clues."

"Do you think—," Becca began.

At that moment I heard a clang from the stairwell. I spun around and saw Alan standing on the top step of the flight coming up from below. He was staring up at Becca and me with a strange expression on his face.

"Alan!" I blurted out, cutting off the rest of Becca's comment. "I—uh—didn't hear you coming."

I hadn't seen Alan Thomas coming the first time I'd met him either. Had that really happened only a few short weeks ago? I'd been having lunch with Bess and George at one of our favorite cafés near River Heights University. Suddenly Alan had appeared beside our table, drooling over Bess and begging her to go out with him.

It wasn't the first time that type of thing had happened. But it was the first time Bess had said yes. She said it was because she saw something different in Alan. He was different, all right. He was outgoing and cheerful and kind of excitable—nerdy, as George liked to call it. I guess that worked for Bess, because the two of them had been together ever since.

Then Becca had called, begging me and my friends to come solve her mystery. Our cover story was that we'd won the cruise in a contest. When Alan found out we would be staying in a luxury four-bedroom suite, he'd practically begged to come along. He was an environmental studies major at the university, and this trip was supposed to give him a head start on his sophomore year research project. That was nice for him, but it made things kind of complicated for the rest of us. See, Becca had sworn us to secrecy— we weren't supposed to tell a soul why we were really onboard the *Arctic Star*. Not even Alan. Had I just blown our cover?

"Nancy! I've been looking all over for you!" Alan exclaimed, hurrying toward me. "Did you get lost on the way to the bathroom or something? You're missing some amazing views."

"Nope, I was just chatting with Becca, that's all." I forced a smile, studying Alan's face. Had he overheard what Becca and I were talking about? His gray eyes looked as guileless as ever. Or did they? Something about the way they were peering into mine made me wonder just how much he'd heard while coming up the stairs. . . .

I dismissed the thought as quickly as it came. Alan was pretty much an open book. Like I said, he'd declared his adoration of Bess the first time they'd met. In fact, he seemed to blurt out pretty much every thought that entered his head. If he'd heard anything important, I'd know it.

"We'd better get back out there," I told him, still smiling. "I don't want to miss any more scenery."

"Smile and say Alaska!" Alan sang out.

Bess giggled, tossing back her blond hair as the sea breeze whipped it across her face. "No way," she said. "If I say that, my face will look funny. I'll stick with the traditional." She struck a pose leaning against the gleaming brass railing, with the Skagway shoreline behind her. "Cheese!"

Alan snapped the photo. "Gorgeous!" he exclaimed, hurrying over to let Bess check out the screen on his digital camera.

George rolled her eyes. "Are we going to stand around here taking pictures all day, or are we actually going to get off this ship and *do* something?" she grumbled.

I grabbed her arm and pulled her aside, dodging a few excited passengers who were rushing toward the gangplank leading to the dock below. "Leave Alan alone for a sec," I said quietly. "I've been dying to tell you what Becca just told me."

"What?" George immediately looked interested. Shooting a quick glance at Alan to make sure he wasn't close enough to hear us, she lowered her voice. "Was it about Vince and Lacey? Did they finally fess up to leaving that nasty note in your luggage?"

Right. That was another unexplained occurrence from earlier in the cruise. The note had read, *I HOPE U GET LOST JUST LIKE UR BAG—& THAT U STAY LOST!*

"No. But the cops caught the jewelry thief." I quickly filled her in.

When I was finished, George let out a low whistle. "So it wasn't anyone from the ship? That's weird."

"I know, right? There's no way he got through security on his own." I glanced over at the exit station set up near the gangplank. Several crew members were there, dressed in Superstar's crisp navy-and-silver uniforms, running ship IDs through a scanner as passengers disembarked for the day's shore stop. Even though the area around the exit was chaotic, with dozens of excited passengers shouting and laughing and eager to start their day in Skagway, the ship's staff maintained perfect order, channeling each person through the scanner station before ushering him or her down the gangplank. Watching the well-organized procedure made it seem impossible that anyone could board unscanned or undetected.

"So who helped him get aboard?" George wondered. "He must have an accomplice, right? A crew member, or maybe another passenger?"

Instead of answering, I cleared my throat loudly. "Get any good shots?" I asked Alan, who was coming toward us with Bess on his heels.

"Of course." Alan winked. "It's easy to get good shots when you have such a beautiful model."

George smirked. She doesn't have much patience for gooey romantic talk. Especially when it came from Alan. "Enough with the photo session," she said. "Let's get off this boat and have some fun."

"Speaking of fun," Bess said as we all wandered

toward the exit station, "what's on the agenda for today?"

"You girls weren't there when Scott came around at lunch yesterday, so I signed us up for a few things," Alan said. He glanced around. "Where is Scott, anyway? He said I should check in with him about the exact schedule."

"I don't see him." I scanned the exit area, which was growing more crowded by the second. Half a dozen raucous redheads—members of a large family reunion—had just entered. I also spotted a few other familiar faces. But I didn't see the lean, tanned form of Scott, the shore excursion specialist, anywhere.

A statuesque blond woman in a Superstar uniform saw me looking around and stepped toward me. "May I help you, Ms. Drew?" she asked in a husky voice heavily shaded with an eastern European accent.

"Oh, hi, Tatjana." I smiled at her, though I couldn't help a flash of unease. Tatjana worked for Becca, and she'd almost caught the two of us discussing the case a couple of times. "Um, we were just looking for Scott so we could check about today's trips."

"He is already onshore," Tatjana replied. "You should be able to find him on the dock once you've disembarked."

"Okay, thanks," Bess said with a smile. "Come on, guys. We'd better get in line."

We headed across the lobby. "Look, it's the ABCs," Alan said, nodding toward three gray-haired women at the back of the line. Alice, Babs, and Coral were experienced cruisers who were seated at our table at dinner.

"And Tobias," George added with considerably less enthusiasm.

I couldn't help a slight grimace myself when I saw the eight-year-old boy. He was pulling at his mother's hand as she and her husband chatted with the three older women.

"Looks like Coral has forgiven him for scaring her half to death with that pet tarantula of his," Bess whispered with a smirk.

"I guess so." I'm not scared of spiders, but I still shuddered a little as I recalled the incident. Tobias had smuggled his tarantula onto the ship, and the hairy eight-legged critter had ended up crawling over the pastries one day at lunch. "That's only fair, though," I added. "Vince and Lacey stole Hazel and put her on the buffet, remember? Tobias didn't have anything to do with it." I shrugged. "Well, unless you count sneaking the spider onboard in the first place . . ."

I let my voice trail off, since we'd reached the group by now. The ABCs and Tobias's parents greeted us cheerfully. Tobias himself ignored us. That was typical. He'd made it clear from the start that he didn't want to be on the cruise, and his attitude generally varied from sullen to downright obnoxious.

"Do you young people have some exciting shore activities planned for today?" Babs inquired.

"I guess so." George shot a look at Alan. "You'll have to ask our own personal event planner."

Alan grinned and swept into a goofy bow. "At your service."

"Are you taking that scenic train trip through the mountains?" Tobias's mother asked. "We're really looking forward to that, aren't we, Tobias?"

"I guess." Tobias shrugged, looking less than

enthusiastic. "Hey, here comes Hiro. He probably wants me to go on some boring tour with him or something."

Sure enough, the youth activities coordinator, a young man in navy shorts and a silver-piped polo shirt, was wandering toward us. He spotted Tobias and waved.

"Have fun onshore, Tobias!" he called. "I'll see you for movie night tonight, right?"

"Whatever." Tobias waved back, then turned to peer at the line in front of us. "When are we getting off this stupid ship, anyway?"

"Patience, Tobias," his mother said. "We have to wait our turn."

Luckily, that didn't take long. A few minutes later we were all making our way down the long gangplank together.

Bess shaded her eyes against the bright morning sun. "This place looks pretty cool."

"Oh, it's supposed to be wonderful," Coral assured her. "Skagway was an important site during the Klondike gold rush in the late 1800s. The main street is supposed to look like a postcard straight out of that time. We can't wait to see it!"

"Sounds like fun, eh, son?" Tobias's father clapped the boy on the back. "Well, have a nice day, everyone. We'll see you back on—"

"Sir! Excuse me, sir!"

We all turned. A young man in a tidy navy-and-silver uniform was running down the gangplank, apologizing profusely as he pushed past other passengers. He looked familiar, and when he got closer, I realized he was one of the busboys from the main dining room.

He skidded to a stop in front of Tobias's father. "I'm so glad I caught you," he said breathlessly, holding up a camera. "You left this in the café after breakfast. I'm sure you'll want it with you today."

Tobias's father's eyes widened. "I hadn't even noticed!" he exclaimed, taking the camera. "Thank you so much, young man. You're right, I'm sure I'll want to take lots of pictures today." He fished a couple of bills out of his pocket. "Thank you for tracking me down."

"Thank *you*, sir." The busboy blushed slightly, then

pocketed the money. He glanced around at the rest of us. "I hope you all enjoy your day in Skagway."

As he turned toward the gangplank, another man rushed down. "Sanchez! There you are," he barked out, grabbing the busboy by the arm. "Come with me. *Now.*"

My friends were already moving down the dock, chatting with the ABCs. But something about the second man's behavior made me curious. I took a step after him as he dragged the busboy to a quiet spot behind a trash bin.

"What is it, boss?" the busboy asked, sounding confused and a little scared.

No wonder. The second man's face was livid. It was obvious he was trying to keep his temper under control, but he wasn't having much luck.

"I'll tell you what it is," he exclaimed, jabbing a finger at the busboy's chest. "You're fired, that's what!"

CHAPTER TWO

In the Line of Fire

"WHAT?" THE BUSBOY'S FACE WENT PALE. "Why? What did I do, boss?"

"You know what you did. You just thought we'd never find out." The boss glared at him.

I winced, feeling sorry for the busboy. He started to protest, looking confused and terrified, and his boss responded, though their voices were too low for me to hear what they were saying anymore. I glanced around for my friends, wondering if they'd noticed what was going on.

Instead I saw a heavyset man with a droopy mustache

hurrying over. I didn't know his name, but I'd seen him a few times on the ship. I assumed he was another passenger, since he always wore a Hawaiian shirt and shorts rather than a navy-and-silver uniform. But he seemed to spend a lot of time hanging around with the staff.

Right now he was zeroing in on the busboy and his boss. "What's going on over here?" he demanded as he rushed up to them. "Is there a problem?"

The boss dropped his hold on the younger man's arm. "It's nothing to worry about, sir," he said smoothly, though his brow was still creased in anger. "Please enjoy your day in Skagway."

Mr. Hawaiian Shirt ignored him, peering at the busboy's anxious face. "You okay, son?" he said. "Because if there's some sort of trouble, you've got to speak up for yourself."

The busboy's face went red. He glanced from his boss to the other man. "It's nothing," he muttered.

"That's right," his boss put in. "Thanks for your concern, sir. Now if you'll excuse us—"

I guess I was staring as all this went on. Because just then, the busboy turned and met my eye. He spun toward his boss.

"It's not right!" he said suddenly, his fists clutched at his sides. "I don't know anything about any illegal drugs! Whoever said they found them in my locker is lying."

"Drugs?" Mr. Hawaiian Shirt barked out. "What's this all about?"

By now the raised voices were attracting attention, even on the busy Skagway dock. Some of the passengers who were disembarking nearby were looking over, and a moment later I saw the tall, broad-shouldered form of the *Arctic Star*'s captain striding in our direction.

"What's going on over here?" Captain Peterson asked. Glancing from the red-faced busboy to Mr. Hawaiian Shirt, he frowned. "Never mind, don't tell me. Let's take this back to the ship. Now." He grabbed the boss by the elbow and the busboy by the shoulder, steering both men toward the gangplank.

"Wait!" Mr. Hawaiian Shirt hurried after them. But he was cut off by a group of laughing redheaded children from the family reunion. By the time he dodged around them, the captain and the two employees had disappeared into the ship.

I caught up to him by the foot of the gangplank. "Wow, what was that all about?" I asked in what I hoped was a friendly, casually curious tone. I stuck my hand out. "By the way, I'm Nancy. Nancy Drew. I've seen you around the ship, remember?"

"Uh, sure." The man glanced at me and shook my hand, though he looked distracted. "Nice to meet you. Fred Smith."

"So what do you think was going on with those two?" I said. "Can you believe that guy fired the busboy in front of everyone? Crazy, right?"

"Just business as usual, I suppose. Excuse me." Fred Smith pulled a cell phone out of his pocket. He hit a button and pressed the phone to his ear, turning away and disappearing into the crowd.

Okay, so much for that. I looked around for my friends. They were a few yards down the dock, gathered around Scott, the shore excursion specialist.

"Where'd you disappear to?" George asked when I joined them.

"Nowhere. Remember that nice busboy with the dimples who cleaned up the drink Coral spilled last night?" I said. "I think he just got fired."

Scott glanced at me. "You talking about Sanchez?" he asked. "Yeah, just heard about that. Something about finding drugs in his locker."

"Really? Wow, crazy," Alan commented.

Scott shrugged. "It happens. Just an unfortunate side effect of dealing with a large crew of workers from all different backgrounds." He grimaced slightly. "Some of them less, um, savory than others. Like Sanchez, for instance." He cleared his throat and pasted a pleasant smile on his face, as if realizing he'd said too much. "In any case, I hope you won't let this incident spoil your day here in Skagway."

"Don't worry about that." George glanced toward the town's main street, which was lined with old-timey buildings. "This place looks pretty cool so far. Now, about that train ride . . ."

The others went back to discussing the day's activities. I was only half listening, though. Could the incident I'd just witnessed have anything to do with our case? That man, Fred Smith, had been one of our suspects the last time around. It was strange how he always seemed to be nearby whenever there was trouble. Did he need to go back on the list? Or could the busboy himself be the jewelry thief's accomplice? Scott had all but come out and said the guy might have a questionable past.

I chewed my lower lip, trying to figure out how all the clues might fit together. I wished I could question Scott about the busboy, since he seemed to know him. But I couldn't, not with Alan standing right there. I didn't want to raise his suspicions by seeming too interested in something like that—especially if he'd heard any of what Becca and I had been talking about earlier.

Come to think of it, I wasn't sure I wanted to raise Scott's suspicions either. Becca and Captain Peterson were still the only two people on the ship who knew why my friends and I were really there. And I wanted to keep it that way. I'd already come close to blowing my cover with Scott back in Ketchikan. I'd seen him sneak out of a tourist show to meet with a seedy-looking guy with a big scar on his face. That had made me suspicious enough to tail him through town, but he'd caught me following him—right as he'd met up with another tough-looking man and handed over a wad of cash. He hadn't been happy about seeing me, since he'd explained he was paying off some gambling debts, which could get him in trouble if the captain found out about them.

I sighed, rubbing my face and stifling a yawn. I hadn't had enough sleep last night, and it was making it hard to focus. Besides, there wasn't much I could do to find out more about the firing right now. I'd just have to ask Becca about it later.

"Smile!" Alan sang out, snapping another picture.

I forced a smile. Bess, George, and I were posing in front of a big black-and-red train car on display in a little park. A sign explained that it was a rotary snowplow, built in 1899 to clear Alaska's heavy snows off the tracks.

After Alan took a couple of more photos, Bess checked her watch. "Hey, does anyone remember what time we need to be at the station for the scenic train ride?" she said. "Was it twelve or twelve thirty?"

George gave her a strange look. No wonder. Bess has a memory like an elephant. She rarely forgets a name, a face, or anything else.

But Alan lowered his camera. "I don't know," he said. "Maybe we'd better double-check."

"Thanks, sweetie." Bess tilted her head and smiled up at him. "We'll wait for you right here while you run over there."

Alan blinked. "Oh. Okay, I'll be right back."

As he hurried off, Bess turned to me. "All right, Nancy," she said briskly. "You've been walking around in a fog for the past hour. What are you thinking about?"

I grinned weakly. "I'm that obvious?"

"Oh, yeah." George leaned back against the snowplow sign, watching as Tobias and his mother posed for a photo his father was taking. "So spill."

I glanced around to make sure nobody was close enough to hear us. The area was crowded with visitors, mostly passengers from our ship and the two others currently docked in Skagway. I wasn't surprised that my friends had noticed I was a little distracted. My mind wouldn't stop buzzing around the incident on the dock. Did it mean something? I couldn't decide.

"I was thinking about that busboy," I said. "It's probably not related to the case, but you never know, right?"

"I guess." Bess looked dubious.

"How would something like that be related?" George asked, sounding even more doubtful.

I frowned. "I don't know, okay? I just want to make sure we don't miss any clues, or—" I cut myself off with a yawn.

"Sorry, are we keeping you up?" George said with a smirk.

I almost snapped back at her, but I swallowed the retort. "Sorry. Guess I'm pretty tired. My wake-up call got messed up this morning, remember?"

The suite where we were staying had its own butler, an enthusiastic, outgoing young man named Max. One of his duties was handling our daily wake-up calls, and that morning he'd entered my room at five a.m. on the dot.

"I *know* I requested a seven thirty wake-up call," I murmured, stifling another yawn.

"Whatever, everyone makes mistakes." George shrugged. "Max said it was just a text mix-up or something, right? And he apologized like crazy for, like, the entire morning."

Bess nodded. "I don't know why you didn't just go back to sleep, Nancy."

"I tried. But your boyfriend was snoring so loudly next door that I couldn't."

"So *that's* why you're so cranky today," George muttered.

I shot her a look. "That, and I still can't believe you knocked my bagel on the floor yesterday at breakfast."

George protested. "I told you that wasn't my fault. Alan totally bumped into my arm!"

"Yeah, yeah," Bess put in. "It's always Alan's fault with you, isn't it, George?"

"Shh," I said as I saw Alan hurrying toward them. "Speak of the devil . . ."

That was the end of any private talk for the moment. We wandered around town, sightseeing and shopping for souvenirs and snacks, until it was time to head back to the station for our scenic train excursion.

"Wow, this is cool," Bess said as we entered the old-fashioned train car. "It's like stepping back in time."

I nodded, though I wasn't paying much attention. I'd spotted a couple of our fellow passengers from the *Arctic Star* in the car. One of them was young travel blogger Wendy Webster. As usual, she stood out in the crowd in her plaid skirt, tank top, and long scarf. She looked up from her laptop computer and spotted us.

"Hey, guys!" she called, shoving her oversize black-framed glasses up her nose and waving. "Is this place epic or what?"

"Sure, if you say so," George said. "Totally epic."

Hearing shouts of laughter from the other end of

the car, I glanced that way. Hiro was seated there, surrounded by about half a dozen kids from the *Arctic Star*, though I noticed Tobias wasn't among them.

"Dibs on the window seat." George pushed past me and flopped into the seat. I sat down next to her, while Bess and Alan sat down in front of us.

Soon the train was winding its way into the mountains. The scenery was so incredible that it actually woke me up a little. The train chugged along the tracks, which wound their way up steep inclines and across rusty iron bridges, all the while revealing stunning views of foothills blanketed with dense evergreen forests, rivers cutting through mountain passes, and distant peaks still dusted in snow even though it was summer.

Eventually, though, my mind started to wander. I glanced ahead at Wendy, who was snapping photos and oohing and aahing along with everyone else. She'd been one of our original suspects too. That had made sense at the time. We'd thought she might be drumming up readers for her blog by creating weird happenings to write about.

But now? Was she still a viable suspect? What would she have to gain by smuggling a jewelry thief onboard? Money, I supposed. Everyone liked money, right? Then again, by that logic, *everyone* could be a suspect. . . .

I shook my head, which was feeling fuzzy and sleepy again. "Be right back," I told George. "I want to go get some fresh air."

"Uh-huh." George was peering at the little screen on her camera and didn't even glance over as I stood up.

I made my way down the aisle, swaying side to side with the motion of the train. At the end of the car, a door led on to the little open-air platform between our car and the next. I stepped out there and took a deep breath of the cool, clean mountain air. I had the platform to myself for the moment, so I stepped over to the railing and looked out. It was kind of a scary view. The train was hugging the side of the mountain on a ledge so narrow I couldn't see the edge of it when I looked down. I'm not normally afraid of heights, but I gulped when I saw the dizzying drop-off to the valley floor far, far below.

Suddenly the door to the next car burst open, and someone stomped out onto the platform. It was Scott, the shore excursions guy. He had a cell phone pressed to his ear.

". . . and you'd better figure out a way to fix things before I get to Anchorage," he hissed into the phone, his voice practically seething with fury. "Because if you don't, I'm going to—"

He cut himself off abruptly as he noticed me standing there, staring at him. Clicking the phone off, he glared at me. His face was twisted with anger, making him look like a completely different person than usual.

He took a quick step toward me. I clutched the railing behind me—the only thing between me and a two-hundred-foot drop to my certain death.

"You!" Scott growled. "What are *you* doing out here?"

CHAPTER THREE

Rebuilding the List

I SUCKED IN A DEEP BREATH, READY TO scream for help. At that moment the door to my train car flew open.

"Nancy!" Bess exclaimed. "There you are." She rushed out, with Alan and George right behind her.

"I told you she went outside," George said.

Alan grinned. "Okay, but you weren't too sure," he teased. "All we knew was that we turned around and she was gone!"

I looked at Scott. His face had relaxed into its usual

calm, jovial expression. He caught me looking and smiled sheepishly.

"Sorry if I startled you, Nancy," he said. "You startled me, too. I guess that's what I get for trying to do two things at once, huh?" Dropping his phone into his shirt pocket, he reached for the door. "Enjoy the scenery, folks."

As he left, Alan tugged at my arm. "Check it out. I want to get a shot of you guys standing here when we pass that waterfall up ahead," he said. "Hurry, Nancy— get over there between Bess and George."

I obeyed, though I wasn't focused on the scenery. I'm not the type of person who gets rattled easily, but Scott had really scared me for a second. The depth of anger in his eyes had been terrifying. Could there be a dark side to him? Maybe a *criminal* side? I'd asked Becca about his background after the incident in Ketchikan, and she'd assured me he was an industry veteran who'd been recommended by Captain Peterson himself. That had been enough to make me cross him off the suspect list then. Was it time to investigate him a little further now?

I wished I could talk to both my friends about it. As it was, the best I could hope for was talking to one of them. As we wandered back toward our seats, I poked Bess in the shoulder.

"This train ride is really romantic, isn't it?" I said meaningfully. "It's nice that you and Alan are getting to enjoy it together."

Bess got the hint right away. "Come to think of it, it's a little crowded around here to call it romantic." She linked her arm through Alan's and peered up at him with a smile. "Should we go find the caboose and take some pictures there? Just the two of us?"

"Sure, Bess. Your wish is my command."

Soon they were heading out the door toward the back of the train. I grabbed George and pulled her in the opposite direction, stopping when we reached a block of empty seats a couple of cars up.

"Very smooth," George said. "Good thing Alan's so clueless. He obviously doesn't even realize we keep trying to ditch him."

"Yeah." I glanced around, double-checking to

make sure we wouldn't be overheard. It seemed pretty safe. Our closest neighbors were a pair of senior citizens snoozing in their seats several rows away. There were also a few members of that family reunion huddled at the windows up near the front of the car, but the clanking, chugging sounds of the train drowned out their conversation. "So listen," I told George, "something happened right before you found me just now. . . ."

I filled her in on the incident with Scott. George looked surprised.

"Shore Excursion Scott?" she said. "You really think *he* could be our bad guy?"

"I don't know." I sighed, leaning back in my seat and staring out the window at the looming mountains. "But he was obviously angry with whoever he was talking to on the phone. What if it had something to do with that robbery?"

"What if it didn't?" George countered. "You said he mentioned fixing something before he got to Anchorage. That's the ship's next stop, remember? He was probably just doing business, organizing the buses to take us from the ship to the city, something like that."

"Maybe." I flashed back to the moment he'd lunged toward me. "But if you could've seen his face when he realized I'd heard him . . ."

"Okay, there's that." George leaned past me to snap a photo of a picturesque mountain pass. "But Becca said he has a good rep, right?"

"Uh-huh. She said the captain recommended him for this job. And he's worked in the cruise industry for quite a while."

George nodded. "Okay. The other thing is, you admitted yourself that you're sleep deprived today. You're probably a little on edge from that. Totally understandable, right? But isn't it possible it's making you freak out over something that's not really freak-out-worthy?"

I couldn't help smiling at her choice of words. "Maybe," I admitted, stifling yet another yawn. "Still, we both know from experience that you can't always tell who's a criminal based on their public reputation. Or even who their friends are." I flashed momentarily to that hulking tough guy Scott had met in Ketchikan, and the man with the scarred face he'd talked to briefly before that. He'd claimed they were poker buddies. Was he telling the truth? "It might be worth checking him out a little more," I added. "Just in case."

"Agreed." George frowned. "Although I'm starting to wonder whether this jewelry robbery business is even worth stressing over. I mean, the cops are already on the case, right? They're way better equipped to handle this kind of investigation—you know, the kind with real criminals. Possibly *dangerous* criminals."

"Yeah, I guess," I said. "But if there's someone on the ship involved—"

"Then the cops will figure it out." George shrugged. "That's their job. Besides, it was probably that busboy we saw get fired earlier. So we could be doing all this investigating and sneaking around for nothing."

"Maybe." I wasn't quite as convinced as she seemed to be. After all, neither the busboy nor his boss had mentioned anything about the robbery—just the illegal drugs. "But even if that busboy *is* the robber's accomplice, we still don't know who left me that threatening note. That couldn't have been the busboy—he'd never even laid eyes on me at that point."

"How do you know the busboy didn't leave the note?" George countered, tapping her foot against the seat in front of us. "You're famous, you know. Sort of, anyway."

I cocked an eyebrow at her. "How do you figure?"

"How many times have you been written up in the papers back home in River Heights for solving mysteries big and small?" George said. "All those stories end up on the newspapers' websites, you know. For all the world to see with a quick web search. So maybe your rep as the Sherlockina Holmes of the Midwest preceded you, and that busboy thought you were coming to Alaska to investigate him. He might have been trying to scare you off before you got started."

"Sounds a little far-fetched, but I suppose anything's possible." I shook my head. "Until we know for sure, we've got to keep our eyes open. I mean, I know we thought the case was closed when we caught Vince and Lacey."

"But they swore they didn't do some of the bad stuff," George said with a nod. "Like pushing you off that walkway in Ketchikan, and the moose antler thing, and some of the problems Becca told us about from before the cruise started."

"Yeah. A few of those incidents could've been accidents or red herrings," I said. "Maybe somebody just bumped me innocently on that narrow walkway, and I lost my balance. And maybe there was an oversight and the screws on that moose antler never got tightened properly, so it fell when Bess and Alan leaned on it."

"And maybe the pre-cruise problems were just bad luck or human error or whatever," George went on.

"Right. But *someone* left that note in my suitcase. And if that same someone might possibly have been the one who pushed me over the railing back in Ketchikan, I need to figure out who it is before something even worse happens. If it turns out that busboy was behind it all like you said, cool. All we've lost is some time and energy we could've used for sightseeing today." I shrugged. "If not? Then we'd better not waste an entire day looking at pretty scenery and shopping for souvenirs while the real culprit could be planning his or her next move."

George didn't answer for a moment, instead clearing her throat loudly. Glancing up, I saw Hiro hurrying down the aisle. He spotted us, too, and smiled.

"Having a nice time?" he asked, pausing and leaning a hand on the back of our seat. "The scenery is spectacular out here, isn't it? I thought I'd miss the warm blue waters of the Caribbean when I left Jubilee to take this job. But it's been great to see a new part of the world."

"You worked for Jubilee before?" I was surprised, though I wasn't sure why. The cruise industry was really pretty small, and Jubilee Cruise Lines was one of its largest players. A lot of the *Arctic Star*'s crew, including Becca, had worked for Jubilee before being lured away by Superstar Cruises.

Hiro nodded. "I was assistant cruise director on one of the ships," he said. "It was a great job, but when I heard Superstar had a spot open for kiddie coordinator, I jumped at it. I love working with kids." He checked his watch. "Speaking of which, I'd better scoot. Got a bunch of the little rascals waiting for me right now. Enjoy the rest of the ride, ladies."

"Thanks," George and I chorused as he hurried off.

"That's weird," George said once he was gone.

"What?" I asked.

She shrugged. "Becca's the assistant cruise director on our ship, right? And I thought you said she was Hiro's boss. So it sounds like he took a demotion to take this job. Why would someone do that? Especially since it sounds like he was skeptical about leaving the Caribbean to come to Alaska?"

"Good question. But I'm not totally sure Becca is actually his boss," I said. "I'll text her right now and ask."

I pulled out my phone and started tapping out a quick text. "Cool, your phone's working again," George said, peering over my shoulder.

"Uh-huh." My phone had gone dead—or at least temporarily unconscious—after my unplanned dip in the cold waters beneath that walkway in Ketchikan. "After it dried out, it was fine."

"So are you going to ask Becca about Scott, too?" George asked.

"I think I'll wait and ask her about that in person." I tucked the phone away. "Seems too complicated to do via text. Anyway, I guess this means Hiro's still on the suspect list?"

"Definitely," George said. "He was around when the moose antler crashed. And you said Becca acted weird when you asked about him that time—maybe she's suspicious of him too."

"Maybe." I thought about that conversation. As soon as I'd mentioned Hiro's name, Becca had rushed off, claiming she needed to be somewhere. "But if she thinks we should investigate him, why wouldn't she just say so?"

"Got me." George shrugged. "Anyway, we already know Scott's on the list now too. Who else?"

I thought about our previous suspect list. "Well, there's Wendy."

"Wendy the Wacko?" George nodded. "Yeah, she's too weird *not* to keep on the list, I guess. But actually,

I'm thinking it's more likely to be a crew member than a passenger. Like Scott or Hiro. Or maybe Tatjana—we were suspicious of her before, right? I mean, how would someone like Wendy sneak around the ship causing trouble? She doesn't exactly blend into the background."

"True. But Wendy still has a decent motive," I said. "She really wants her blog to be a success. What better way than making sure this cruise is one everybody wants to read about, even if it's a crime she's writing about?" I remembered one more suspect we hadn't discussed yet. "And let's not forget Fred."

"Fred? Who's Fred?"

"Mr. Hawaiian Shirt," I said. "I forgot to tell you, he turned up right after the busboy got fired and started trying to get involved."

"Weird. The guy acts like he'd rather be working on the ship than traveling on it," George said. "Pretty sure I've seen him in the kitchen more often than I've seen him at the pool."

"Yeah." I didn't say anything else, mostly because about a dozen redheads were pouring into the train car. They were all chatting and laughing, and several of them were clutching cameras. They rushed over to the other family reunion members, overflowing into the seats near ours.

One of them, a twentyish young woman with an auburn ponytail, glanced at George and me with a smile. "Hi! You're from our ship, right?" she said. "Isn't this fun?"

"Yeah, it's great," George said.

Obviously we'd lost our quiet conversation spot. Probably just as well—if George and I stayed away too long, Alan might get suspicious. Especially if he'd heard even a little of my conversation with Becca earlier. He might be clueless, but he wasn't stupid. I didn't want to give him any excuse to figure out what was going on behind his back. I sure didn't want to risk blowing my cover—for Becca's sake and the safety of the ship's passengers.

I stood up, returning the redhead's smile. "Sorry, I think we took your seats," I told her. "We'd better go find our friends now. See you back on the ship."

"Wait up a sec, guys," George said. "I have to tie my shoe."

"Hurry up," Alan told her as he, Bess, and I stopped. "Scott said we're running late, and I don't want to miss my chance to make my fortune."

Bess grinned, squeezing his hand. "Don't get your hopes up, sweetie," she said. "This gold-panning place is just a tourist spot right here in town. It's not exactly breaking new ground in the next gold rush."

George glanced up from fiddling with the laces of her sneakers. "Still, gold's gold," she said. "Scott said this place guarantees we'll each get to find some real gold in our pans."

"Yeah. Like three granules of gold dust, probably," Bess said.

As they continued squabbling amiably, I glanced forward. We were at the tail end of the large group of *Arctic Star* passengers making its way from the train station to the next activity in Skagway. Scott was at the front, leading the way.

My gaze lingered on him. He was back in professional mode, smiling and helpful, with no hint of the terrifying anger I'd seen. Could George be right? Had my exhaustion—not to mention my obsession with this case—made me see something that wasn't there?

I forgot about that as the crowd shifted and I spotted another familiar figure. It was Fred. He wasn't part of the group heading to the gold-panning place—instead he was scurrying along the sidewalk across the way with his hands in his pockets and his head tucked down between his shoulders. Almost as if he didn't want to be seen. Interesting.

George finally finished tying her shoe. "Come on, let's hurry," she said. "I want to make sure I get the best gold-panning spot."

"You guys go ahead," I said. "I, um, need to find a restroom. I'll meet up with you in a minute."

"You sure?" Alan said teasingly. "Don't expect us not to steal your gold if you take too long, Nancy!"

I forced a smile, trying to keep Fred in view out of the corner of my eye. "I'll have to take my chances. See you in a bit."

By the time I pushed my way through the eager, gold-crazed crowd around me, Fred had disappeared. I hurried off in the direction I'd last seen him going. Whew! I spotted him again as soon as I rounded the next corner. He was just a few yards ahead of me, moving fast.

I fell into step behind him, doing my best to keep a few people between us. Good thing. Halfway down the block, Fred stopped abruptly, then turned and peered behind him. Oops.

Luckily, he didn't seem to see me. But it reminded me to be careful.

I continued to tail him. It wasn't easy. He stopped and stared around suspiciously every few moments. What was he doing?

Finally he ducked into a large souvenir shop. I waited a moment, allowing a few other people to pass before stepping inside myself.

The place was cavernous and crowded, packed with tourists pawing through tables overflowing with

T-shirts, key chains, stuffed animals, and every other imaginable form of souvenir knickknack.

But where was Fred? I glanced around but couldn't see him anywhere. Outside, his brightly colored Hawaiian shirt had made him easy to spot. In here, surrounded by every flavor of colorful tchotchke? Not so much.

I moved deeper into the store, dodging a sticky-looking little girl cooing at a stuffed arctic fox and several loud, excited women with Boston accents exclaiming over some salmon jerky. Still no sign of my quarry.

Then I spotted a flash of orange and red toward the back of the store near an oversize stuffed grizzly bear wearing a Skagway souvenir hat and an apron emblazoned with the Alaskan flag. Hurrying closer, I finally spotted Fred.

He was huddled behind the bear, deep in conversation with Sanchez, the fired busboy!

CHAPTER FOUR

Unpleasant Surprises

MY HEART POUNDED AS I CREPT CLOSER to the stuffed bear. Fred appeared to be doing most of the talking. But he was keeping his voice too low for me to hear what he was saying.

"Nancy! Hey, Nancy! Over here!" a voice yelled loudly, cutting through the din of the souvenir shop.

I glanced back over my shoulder, wincing. It was Wendy the blogger. She was rushing toward me, clutching her laptop under one arm as she used the other to wave vigorously at me.

Biting back a groan of dismay, I quickly turned

toward Fred and the busboy. But they were gone.

By then Wendy had reached me. "Hey, girl," she said breathlessly. "What's up? Shopping for some new shades?" She grinned.

"Huh?" Glancing down at the nearest table, I realized it was filled with garish novelty sunglasses. "No, just looking around." I sneaked another glance around the store, but Fred was nowhere in sight. Had he skedaddled when he'd heard Wendy's bellowing and realized I was watching him? If so, what did that mean? Did he know I was investigating, or was he just trying not to let anyone see him talking to the fired busboy?

"Cool." Wendy grabbed a pair of moose-print socks off another table. "Wow, some of this stuff is tacky."

I wasn't sure she had much room to talk, given her usual crazy thrift-shop style. But I was less concerned with her fashion choices than with her position on my suspect list. Deciding to try to salvage the situation with a little subtle interrogation, I gave her a friendly smile.

"So what are you doing here?" I asked. "I thought

everyone was still down the street learning to be gold panners."

"Oh." Wendy tossed the socks back on the table. "Nah, I did a gold-panning thing like that in California once and it was kind of lame, so I decided to save my pennies this time."

"Oh?" Was it my imagination, or had she briefly grimaced when she'd said the part about saving her pennies?

"Yeah. Figured I'd skip it and see if I could find something a little more interesting to share with my readers."

"So have you found anything yet?" I asked.

She grinned, waggling a finger in my face. "Nuh-uh, not telling!" she singsonged. "You'll just have to check out my blog to find out."

"Guess I'll have to do that," I said politely.

"Really?" she said eagerly. "Cool! Tell all your friends to go there too, okay? Because so far, this trip isn't exactly driving zillions of hits to the blog. I knew I should've done the Elvis pilgrimage to Graceland this time instead."

Interesting. So her blog, Wendy's Wanderings, wasn't exactly setting the Internet on fire these days. Was that suspicious? I wasn't sure, though I supposed it did make Wendy's theoretical motive even stronger.

Before I could come up with any more questions, Wendy's eyes lit up. "Whoa, check that out!" she exclaimed, racing toward a nearby table full of earrings. I didn't understand why she was so excited until I read the sign, which explained that the earrings were made of moose droppings. Wendy pulled a camera out of her pocket and snapped a few photos. "That's so going on the blog," she murmured gleefully.

As she started digging through the earrings, I decided to take the opportunity to exit stage right. "See you later," I said, hurrying off before she could answer.

Once I was back out on the street, I texted Becca to see if she was available to meet with me. She texted back almost immediately, saying she was free for a few minutes if I could meet her back on the ship.

Soon I was hurrying into a snack bar on one of the *Arctic Star*'s middle decks. Becca was sitting at a table with her laptop open in front of her. She glanced up when I came in and waved me over. A handsome young man was bustling around behind the counter, but otherwise the place was a ghost town. Actually, the whole ship was all but deserted. Other than the employees who'd swiped my ID and checked me in, the only person I'd seen since boarding was a maid vacuuming one of the hallways.

"Hi," I said, sitting down across from Becca. "You know, this ship is kind of creepy when it's empty." My words echoed in the almost deserted snack bar.

"I know what you mean. The ship feels different without passengers. Kind of peaceful, and yes, maybe a little creepy." Becca snapped her laptop shut.

Meanwhile, the young bartender had just come around from behind the counter. He was carrying a pair of tall, frosty glasses of iced tea.

"There you go, ladies," he said, setting the drinks down in front of us. "Anything else?"

"Thanks, Omar." Becca smiled at him. "And yes,

actually, could you do me a favor? Marcelo's up in his office, and I know he'd love a cup of coffee. Would you mind bringing him one?"

"Sure thing."

As the young man hurried out, coffee cup in hand, Becca winked at me. "Okay, now we can talk freely. At least until he gets back."

I grinned. "Nicely done. I didn't realize you had such a talent for misdirection and deception. Have you ever considered leaving the cruise industry and going into undercover work?"

Becca chuckled, but soon her face went serious again. "So what did you want to talk about, Nancy? Are we any closer to figuring out who helped that robber get onboard?"

"I don't know." I took a sip of my iced tea. "But I have a question for you. What do you know about the busboy who got fired this morning?"

"John Sanchez?" Becca nodded. "How did you know about that?"

I explained about the scene I'd witnessed on the dock. "So now I'm wondering if there's a connection," I finished.

Becca shook her head. "That wasn't very professional," she said with a sigh. "Chuck must have been too upset to wait until they were back onboard. I know he thinks of his entire staff as family."

"Chuck?" I echoed.

"Sanchez's boss," Becca explained. "He got an anonymous tip this morning advising him to check the guy's locker. When he did, he found the drugs hidden under a spare apron."

"An anonymous tip?"

"Yeah, apparently someone e-mailed him from one of the public computers in the ship's Internet café," Becca said. "The message wasn't signed. Why? Do you think any of this is connected with the case?"

"I'm not sure yet." I tucked the info away to think about later. I knew we might not have much time before the bartender came back, and I wanted to ask her all my questions. "I also wanted to talk to you about Scott again. You know—the shore excursions guy. You said he's got a good rep in the industry, but how well do you really know him?"

Becca shrugged. "Not that well. I never met him before he got hired here. All I know is he used to work for Happy Seas Cruises, and his old boss put in a good word for him with Captain Peterson. Why? Has Scott done something suspicious? You asked about him before, right?"

"Maybe. I don't know. Sort of." The more time passed after the incident on the train, the more I doubted my own reaction. Was I grasping at straws by treating Scott as a viable suspect?

"Okay." Becca checked her watch, then glanced toward the door. "But listen, Omar will be back any second, and I want to talk to you about something."

"What is it?" I asked, a little distracted by my own thoughts.

"It's Tatjana. She's been acting, well, kind of strange lately."

Instantly I snapped back to attention. Even though

Tatjana had been on the original suspect list, I hadn't been thinking much about her lately, mostly because my suspicions of her were based on the way she seemed to keep turning up whenever I was discussing the case with Becca. Which really wasn't all that suspicious, given that Becca was her boss.

"What do mean, acting strange?" I asked.

Becca twirled her straw in her iced tea, her expression troubled. "It's probably nothing. It's just that she hasn't been answering calls or texts right away lately. And a couple of times I haven't been able to find her where she was supposed to be—it's like she just disappears now and then. It's not quite enough to put my finger on, but . . ."

"Okay. I'll look into it," I said. "As a matter of fact, Tatjana is—"

I cut myself off as I heard rushing footsteps. Glancing at the door, I expected to see Omar returning. Instead I saw that Hiro had just burst in, red-faced and breathless.

"Hi," he said, looking startled to see us there. "That is, um . . ."

"What are you doing here?" Becca blurted out.

I was surprised to see him too. "I thought you were herding kids at the gold-panning place," I said with a smile.

"That wrapped up a few minutes ago." Hiro returned my smile, though it looked a bit forced. "The passengers are on their own for the rest of the afternoon. Even the little kids."

Becca stood up. "Excuse me," she said, looking strangely uncomfortable. "I just remembered I'm supposed to take care of something before the passengers get back. I'd better go. Talk to you later, Nancy."

"Wait," I said. "I—"

It was too late. She was gone. And Becca had never answered my text about Hiro.

I glanced at Hiro, who was shifting his weight from foot to foot, looking as agitated as one of the hyper little kids he was paid to entertain. Maybe this was another opportunity for some impromptu interrogation.

"Were you looking for Omar or something?" I asked. "He should be right back, if you want to sit down and wait."

"Oh!" Hiro glanced at me with that same forced smile. "That's okay. I was just looking for, um, someone else. Thanks, though."

With that, he darted out the door. I shrugged. Oh well, so much for that. But what was up with Becca? Her behavior reminded me that this wasn't the first time she'd reacted oddly to seeing Hiro. What was that all about?

My phone buzzed, interrupting my thoughts. It was George calling.

"Where are you? Never mind, don't tell me—just get over to the ice cream parlor near the gold-panning place pronto," she hissed. "Alan's driving us crazy asking where you are, and we're running out of excuses. Bess can only distract him for so long by fluttering her eyelashes and laughing at his lame jokes."

I sighed, all thoughts of snooping around the nearly empty ship fleeing my mind. "Be right there," I promised.

"Do we really have to change for dinner?" George complained as we walked down the carpeted hallway toward our suite a few hours later. "I'm starved. And if we don't get there soon, Babs will snarf all the rolls."

"Yes, we do," Bess told her. "We've been walking around all day in summer weather, and we all could use a shower and some fresh clothes." She wrinkled her nose. "Plus I think you spilled half the gold dust you panned down your shirt."

"Really?" George plucked at her T-shirt, trying to get a look at it.

I, for one, was looking forward to showering and changing. After I'd rejoined my friends at the ice cream parlor, we'd spent an hour or so wandering around seeing the sights. Then we'd returned to the ship, where Alan had insisted on finding a spot on one of the upper decks so we could watch the ship pull away from Skagway. By now we were all sunburned and hungry.

Bess reached for the door, but it opened before she could touch the knob. Our butler, Max, stood in the doorway, grinning at us. He was short and wiry, with thick blond hair, dancing blue eyes, and seemingly boundless energy. Upon first meeting him, he'd reminded me of a golden retriever in human form, and my impression hadn't changed since.

"Welcome home!" he exclaimed. "How was Skagway?"

"Great," Alan said. He started telling the butler all about our day as we entered the suite.

I didn't hear much of what he said as I headed for my bedroom. My stomach grumbled as I yanked open a dresser drawer. I was so busy puzzling over everything that had happened that day that it took a moment for me to register that the drawer was empty.

"Huh?" I mumbled, blinking at the sight. Hadn't I folded and put away some shirts in there just that morning?

I opened another drawer above the first one, wondering if I'd stuck the shirts in with my underwear by mistake. Stranger things had been known to happen when I was distracted by a case.

But that drawer was empty too. I checked the other drawers—nothing in any of them. In fact, the only clothes in my room were the ones I'd left in the little built-in hamper near the door.

I stepped outside. The others had disappeared into their own rooms by then, and Max was whistling a cheery tune as he swept the floor.

"Hey, Max," I said. "Do you know what happened to my clean clothes?"

"You mean the ones I sent out for laundering this morning?" he asked brightly. "They should be back first thing tomorrow."

I glanced over my shoulder at the dirty clothes spilling out of my open hamper. "Which ones did you send out?" I asked. "Because my hamper's still full."

"I know." Max shrugged and grinned. "You left me a note right on the hamper, remember?"

"A note?" It had been a very long day since that early wake-up call, and my mind felt sluggish, unable to deal with this new wrinkle. "What note?"

"The one where you said you'd stuck your clean clothes in the hamper and the dirty ones in the drawers, so I should be sure to send out the right ones." Max grinned and winked. "Most guests do it the other way around, but I don't like to judge."

I put a hand to my forehead. "You sent all the clothes in the drawers out to be washed?"

"Yes." Max's smile faded slightly. "Isn't that what you meant by the note?"

"What note?" I said again. "Can I see it?"

"I threw it away." He shrugged. "Why? Is there a problem? I'm sorry if I misunderstood. . . ."

My mind spun, still refusing to take this in. I'd been pretty tired that morning, but I knew I hadn't left Max any notes about my laundry. That meant that one of two things was happening here. One of the possibilities was that Max was lying to me—that there *was* no note. So he'd either sent out the wrong laundry by mistake, or worse yet, on purpose. Was this just another innocent error along with that messed-up wake-up call? Or should he be a suspect? My mind shot from the laundry to the wake-up call to the note in my luggage, trying to work out whether Max could be the accomplice I was looking for.

The other possibility was even more disturbing. Maybe the note was real—which would mean someone had sneaked into our suite and planted it on my laundry hamper. Who would do something so petty and weird? Somehow it didn't fit in with the other incidents we were investigating.

"I'm so sorry, Miss Drew." Max looked stricken now as he realized how upset I was. "Did I do something wrong?"

His voice had risen, both in pitch and volume. Bess stuck her head out of her room. "Is everything okay?" she asked.

"Not exactly . . ." I quickly outlined the problem, with Max interrupting every few lines to apologize. He also offered to run down to the shipboard shops and pick me up something to wear at his expense.

But Bess shook her head. "It's okay," she told both of us. "I've got plenty of clothes. Come on in, Nancy—you can borrow something of mine."

I smiled weakly. "Thanks," I said, following her into her room. "Sometimes it's nice having a friend who's a fashion plate."

The following day I awoke feeling rested and ready for anything thanks to a nice dinner (in one of Bess's dresses) and a full night's sleep (in a T-shirt and sweatpants borrowed from George). My doubly clean laundry was back by the time I got up, plus Max had whisked off the stuff from the hamper, promising to get it washed quickly.

The butler was acting so apologetic about the laundry mix-up that I was starting to doubt my suspicions of him from the night before. I'd had a few minutes to discuss those suspicions with Bess in hurried whispers while she was finding me something to wear, and she'd seemed pretty dubious too. Still, we'd agreed that it was worth adding Max to the suspect list. Why not? It wasn't as if we were any closer to solving this thing.

After a leisurely breakfast, we joined most of the rest of the passengers on the upper decks. The ship was cruising through Glacier Bay today, and we were all expecting some spectacular views.

The scenery didn't disappoint. Soon everyone was oohing and aahing over the jagged icy-blue-and-white glaciers surrounding us, framed by the majestic snow-capped mountains rising in the distance. I even forgot about the case for a while. Then I noticed Wendy wandering past, clutching her camera and her laptop, and it all came crashing back. I bit my lip, wishing I could steal a few minutes to discuss my latest thoughts with my friends. But I couldn't; not with Alan right there.

"Should we try the next deck down?" he asked, leaning over the rail to snap another photo. "There might be better views down there."

"Doubtful," George said. "If you're bored, just say so, dude."

"I'm not bored," Alan answered quickly. He shifted his weight from one foot to the other. "I just don't want to miss anything."

"Tobias!" an irritated voice called out from nearby, distracting me from whatever George said next. "Settle down, son. Let's not bother the other passengers."

Glancing that way, I saw Tobias swinging on a railing. His mother was snapping pictures nearby, while his father glared irritably at the boy.

George was looking that way too. "Looks like you're not the only one with a short attention span, Alan," she said with a laugh.

"Ha-ha, very funny," Alan answered.

Suddenly I had an idea. "Looks like Tobias's poor parents are at the end of their rope," I said, keeping my voice casual. "Too bad Hiro isn't around to take him to get his energy out on the climbing wall. Especially since there's probably nobody else there right now—he could go crazy on that thing."

"Good point, Nancy." Bess turned her big, innocent blue eyes toward Alan. "Maybe you should offer to take him, sweetie. I know you've been dying to try the climbing wall."

That was exactly what I was counting on. Alan had mentioned wanting to try the ship's state-of-the-art rock-climbing wall several times, but as far as I knew, he hadn't done it yet. Probably because Bess had no interest in such things.

"Oh," Alan said, glancing from Bess to the scenery and back again. "Um, I guess that's not a bad idea.

We could just go for a little while—give Tobias's folks a break."

"What a nice idea." Bess squeezed his arm, turning on that million-watt smile of hers that never fails to turn guys into jelly. "Why don't you go suggest it to them? I'm sure they'd really appreciate it."

Moments later Alan and Tobias were disappearing into the nearest stairwell. "Come on," I told Bess and George, heading away from the crowds at the rail. "We need to talk."

Soon the three of us were huddled behind a stack of lounge chairs. I started by filling them in on the previous day's chat with Becca and subsequent encounter with Hiro, since this was my first chance to talk freely to them since then. We discussed all that for a few minutes, though we didn't reach any new conclusions.

"Did you tell George about your newest suspect?" Bess asked.

"You mean Max?" I said.

"Max?" George said. "You're kidding, right? The guy doesn't exactly seem like a hardened criminal."

"I know," I said. "But it's weird how he keeps messing things up lately—and how it always affects me."

"Paranoid much?" George rolled her eyes. "I mean, seriously, Nancy—a botched wake-up call? Sending out the wrong laundry? This is your evidence that he's up to no good?"

"I know, I know." I glanced around to make sure nobody had wandered close enough to hear us. "But what if he's been in cahoots with that jewelry thief all along? He definitely had access to our luggage, which means he could have left that nasty note in my suitcase on the first day. And maybe now he's just trying to distract me however he can, hoping it'll throw me off the case." The argument sounded weak even to my own ears.

"Okay, there's that," Bess said diplomatically. "What about the rest of the suspect list?"

We went on to discuss our other suspects, including Wendy, Scott, Fred, and Tatjana. Could any of them be the thief's accomplice? None of us could come up with any compelling evidence for or against.

"It just doesn't quite add up, does it?" I said at last, leaning against the stack of chairs and squinting up into the cloudless blue sky. "We have a whole bunch of suspects, but not much solid evidence. Just vague clues that could mean anything. We've been investigating for days, and it feels like we're no closer to figuring out who could be the thief's accomplice."

George opened her mouth to respond. Before she could say a word, another voice spoke up from behind us.

"Thief's accomplice?" Alan said. "What the heck are you guys talking about?"

CHAPTER FIVE

Comic Relief

"ALAN!" BESS BLURTED OUT.

Alan looked over the stack of chairs. His forehead was creased in a puzzled frown. "What's going on?" he asked, looking at each of us in turn.

"Um . . ." George gulped. "We were just, ah, role-playing. That's it—we're actually super geeks, and we're really into, um, acting out famous true crimes from history. Now you know our secret—oh well, we're pathetic nerds."

Alan shook his head. "Nice try." He glanced at me. "I thought I was going crazy when I heard you talking to the assistant cruise director about clues and stuff. And now here you are again, discussing suspects and evidence and accomplices. . . ."

Uh-oh. Apparently Alan had overheard more than I'd thought yesterday morning. Added to his accidental eavesdropping just now? Well, it seemed the cat was out of the bag.

I took a deep breath, glancing at my friends. "I guess our secret's out. We'd better fill him in."

"Fill him in?" George echoed cautiously. "Um, you mean . . ."

"The truth," I finished for her. I was annoyed at myself for being so careless, letting him find out more than he should. But besides that? I was mostly, well, relieved. Now we wouldn't have to sneak around behind Alan's back anymore, which should make our lives— and the investigation—much easier. Maybe he'd even be some help.

"Okay, if you say so," Bess said. She turned and took Alan's hands in hers. "I'm sorry we haven't been honest with you. It's only because Becca swore us to absolute secrecy. We didn't win this cruise in a contest. We were called in to look into some mysterious happenings. See, Becca knows Nancy from way back, and when she suspected someone was out to sabotage the *Arctic Star* . . ."

From there, the three of us took turns telling him the whole story. Alan's eyes got wider and wider as we talked. When we finished, he let out a loud puff of breath.

"Wow," he said. "This is insane!" He turned to stare at me. "And you're some big-time girl detective? I had no idea!"

"Yes, you did," Bess said. "I know I mentioned it a couple of times. Remember? When we saw that mystery movie on our third date, I told you Nancy would've had the case solved in half the time."

"Oh, okay, right, I guess you did say something like that." Alan shrugged. "But I didn't think she was so, you know, *serious* about it. I mean, I figured her dad's a hotshot lawyer, so she was probably just goofing around, pretending to investigate his big cases or whatever. . . ."

"Shh," I hissed, noticing Wendy wandering closer, staring down at the screen on her camera. "Incoming."

"Huh?" Alan said, his voice sounding way too loud. "Hang on, I have a question—is this the real reason why Nancy is always running off to the bathroom and stuff?"

Bess pinched him on the arm. "Quiet, then," she murmured. "We have to keep this on the down-low, okay?"

"Oh!" His eyes widened again, and he nodded, shooting a suspicious look around. "I gotcha. Top secret stuff, right?"

I cringed. This was what I'd been afraid of. Alan was so excitable—what if he blurted something out at the wrong time?

Oh well. Whatever happened, we were just going to have to deal with it. Might as well look on the bright side. Four heads were better than three, right? With Alan helping to keep an eye on our suspects, maybe we'd actually crack this case before the end of the trip.

"Come on," I said once Wendy had passed by, luckily without noticing us. "We can talk more back at the suite later. This could be our once-in-a-lifetime chance to check out this awesome scenery."

"Are you sure you want to go to the show?" Alan asked, straightening his tie and glancing into the mirrored wall in the suite's entryway. "Wouldn't you rather take this chance to, you know, sleuth around or whatever while the rest of the passengers are busy?" He waggled his eyebrows meaningfully.

I bit back a sigh. "No, it's fine," I said, double-checking to make sure Max was safely out of earshot in one of the bedrooms. "I'm sure most of our suspects will be there tonight. Two birds with one stone and all that."

"Right." Bess reached up to flick a speck of lint off Alan's sleeve. "Besides, I know you've been looking forward to seeing Merk's show, sweetie."

The idea behind Superstar Cruises was that passengers would get the chance to spend time with the celebrity talent hired as the ship's entertainment. Unfortunately, the *Arctic Star*'s main attraction, A-list action star Brock Walker, had canceled at the last minute due to Vince and Lacey's shenanigans. That had left C-list comedian Merk the Jerk as the ship's headliner. Tonight was his first performance—his original show had been postponed when Vince and Lacey had sabotaged the chandelier in the ship's main theater. Now the place was cleaned up and the show was back on.

"We'd better get moving if we want decent seats," George said, heading for the door. "It's first come, first served."

The theater was already crowded when we arrived, but we still managed to find good seats near the front.

"This is going to be awesome!" Alan rubbed his hands together, leaning forward to peer at the stage. "I heard Merk does a really funny bit about cruise fashions."

"Hmm." I wasn't too interested in speculating about the comedian's set. Instead I was glancing around for our suspects. But I hadn't spotted any of them by the time the lights dimmed.

"Here we go," George whispered.

Becca's boss, Marcelo, stepped out onstage, looking dapper in a dark suit. A smattering of applause greeted his appearance, and he raised both hands and smiled.

"Thank you, thank you," the cruise director said. "I know we're all looking forward to having our funny bone tickled by our wonderful celebrity guest, Merk the Jerk. First, though, the captain would like to say a few words. Sir?"

He turned and swept into a gallant bow. Captain Peterson strode out onstage and shook Marcelo's hand, then took his place at the microphone.

"Good evening, everyone," he said. "Before we get started with tonight's entertainment, I want to fill you in on the schedule for the next few days. As you know, the *Arctic Star* departed Glacier Bay just before dinnertime tonight and is now cruising toward Seward, where we'll dock for a few days while most of you travel by comfortable motor coach to Anchorage to begin the land tour portion of your trip."

He went on to explain that some of the ship's personnel—Scott, Hiro, Tatjana, and several others—would be accompanying us as we visited Anchorage and then traveled north from there to Denali National

Park. The rest of the staff, including Becca, Max, and the captain himself, would stay behind to ready the ship for the return voyage down the coast to Vancouver.

"Yikes," George breathed in my ear. "Sounds like our suspects are splitting up."

I nodded, feeling a pang of concern. At least Max was the only staff member on our list who wouldn't be traveling with the passengers. Still, if he was our culprit, that would mean he'd have plenty of free time to plan more trouble before we returned. And the captain had said "most of" the passengers would be going on the land tour. What if Wendy was planning to save money by skipping it and staying behind on the ship? Or what if Fred decided he'd rather hang out with his pals in the kitchen than go with the rest of us? I wondered whether one of us should stay behind on the ship just in case.

Reaching into my pocket, I touched my phone. Maybe I should text Becca and get her advice about what to do. Before I could decide, the lights dimmed again and raucous music poured out of the speakers. I realized the captain had left the stage, and it was time for Merk's show to start.

The comedian strode out with a cocky grin on his face. "Welcome, ladies and grunts!" he shouted. "I hope you're enjoying your stay on the *Arctic Star*, where the drinks are cold and the passengers are old."

"Ba-*dum*-bum," George said with a grin, while people all around us laughed, booed, or cheered.

The show continued from there. My friends seemed to be enjoying themselves, laughing and clapping and letting out hoots of approval. But I couldn't seem to focus on the comedian's act.

"Be right back," I hissed at George.

Luckily, we were near the end of our row, so I only had to climb over her and a few other people to get out. Soon I was in the hushed, carpeted hallway outside the theater. An older man was out there, fiddling with his hearing aid.

"Funny show, eh?" he said conversationally. "Just wish I could hear it a bit better."

"Yeah, it's great. Excuse me, I need to find the

ladies' room." I smiled at the man, then hurried off around the nearest corner. Pulling out my phone, I started tapping out a message to Becca as I walked.

A moment later, the sound of muffled but excited-sounding voices pulled my attention away from my text. Where was that coming from?

There was a door standing ajar just ahead; the voices were coming from that direction. Curious, I hurried forward and peered in.

The door opened into what looked like some kind of meeting room. About a dozen people were inside, gathered around a large, polished wooden table. Most of them were dressed in ship uniforms, but the person standing at the head of the table was wearing a loud Hawaiian shirt.

Fred looked up and saw me staring in at him. His face twisted into a scowl.

"Why do you keep turning up everywhere I look?" he exclaimed, jabbing a finger in my direction. "If you're spying on me, you'll be sorry!"

CHAPTER SIX

Sharp Questions

"WH-WHAT?" I STAMMERED, TAKEN ABACK. "Spying? Uh, no, sorry, I just . . ." My voice trailed off. The other people in the room had turned to stare at me, and I recognized one of them as Daisy, our usual dinner waitress. "Hi, Daisy," I said, taking a step toward her. "It's me, Nancy."

Daisy was popular with all of us for her bright smile and friendly attitude. But she wasn't displaying either at the moment. "H-hello, Nancy," she said quietly.

"So what's going on in here?" I asked her, and glanced around. "Is everything all right?"

Daisy shot a look at Fred. "Er, nothing," she said quickly. "It's nothing. Everything's fine. We're just listening."

There was a low murmur of assent. None of the other employees were meeting my eye. Then a young man stood up. I was pretty sure he worked as a lifeguard at the pool.

"Nobody here has agreed to anything," he said, his voice quavering. "There's no need to tell our bosses about any of this."

"That's enough," Fred said sharply. "You don't have to tell her anything." He glared at me. "Your cover is blown, young lady," he said, his words dripping with sarcasm.

I froze. Was Fred on to me? "I—I don't know what you—," I began.

He didn't give me a chance to continue. "I've seen you talking with the assistant cruise director more than once. You two looked pretty chummy." He crossed his arms over his chest. "You're working for Superstar, aren't you? Keeping the little people in line? I hope you're proud of yourself!"

My heart rate slowed slightly. "Huh?" I said. "The little people? What are you talking about?"

Fred rolled his eyes dramatically. "You can drop the act. We both know why you're here. But you might as well give up. Unionization is coming—it's right, and you can't stop it."

I blinked, taking that in. "Unionization?" Glancing around at the worried faces staring back at me, I finally realized what was going on here. "You're trying to form a union?"

"Like we said, we're just listening to what he has to say," someone spoke up. "Please don't tell management, or we could lose our jobs."

"Don't worry, I'm not trying to get anyone fired." I turned to Fred. "So you're a union organizer?"

He still looked hostile. "Yeah. As if you didn't know that already."

"I didn't." I shrugged. "I had no idea, actually. And you can all relax—I'm not here to turn you in to management. I had no idea any of this was going on, and as far as I'm concerned, it's none of my business."

"So you're not going to tell?" Daisy asked.

I shook my head. "As long as there's nothing illegal going on here—and it sounds like there's not—your secret's safe with me."

Murmurs of relief came from around the room. Daisy's sunny smile reappeared. "Thanks, Nancy," she said.

"No need to thank me." I smiled back, then returned my attention to Fred. "So this whole time, you've been trying to organize a union?" I said. "That explains why you spend so much time in the kitchen and places like that."

Fred still looked suspicious and a little confused. "Hang tight, people," he told the employees. "I'll be back in a minute." Then he steered me out into the hallway. "So you're really not a management spy?" he asked when we were alone. "Then why are you always talking with Becca Wright? And why do I keep running into you everywhere I turn?"

"Becca's an old family friend," I told him. "As for running into each other, that's bound to happen. This ship is big, but not *that* big."

"Hmm." Fred still didn't look entirely convinced. But he shrugged. "All right, then. You don't really fit the mold, anyway. But when you turned up on the dock in Skagway after John Sanchez got fired, I really started to wonder."

"Yeah, that was weird, wasn't it?" I realized that just because Fred was a union organizer, it didn't necessarily mean he couldn't also be my culprit. I might as well take this opportunity for a little snooping. "But I heard they really did find drugs in his locker."

Fred frowned. "That's what they say. I find it pretty hard to believe."

"Oh? How so?"

"That kid was a model employee. Hardworking, well-liked, no history of any kind of trouble. Definitely no history of being mixed up with drugs." Fred squared his shoulders. "This is exactly why I'm here—to help workers." He looked back into the room. "At least maybe seeing him get axed with no real evidence got some of the others to wake up and listen."

Personally, I wasn't sure that finding illegal drugs

among someone's possessions counted as "no real evidence." But it was pretty obvious that Fred had latched on to the incident and was planning to milk it for all it was worth and then some.

"You could be right," I said. "Then again, there have been some odd things happening on this cruise. Maybe this Sanchez guy had something to do with all that."

"Huh?" Fred looked confused. "What odd things?"

"You know—like the jewelry store getting robbed, and the chandelier falling in the theater," I prompted. Okay, so I already knew that Vince and Lacey had sabotaged the chandelier. I figured it would still be interesting to see his reaction.

"I thought they caught the robber, didn't they? And I heard the chandelier thing was some kind of accident." He chuckled. "Actually, I'm not convinced the thing actually fell at all. Figured Merk the Jerk just felt like lounging by the pool for a few more days instead of doing an honest night's work."

He was already glancing back toward the room behind him. But I wasn't ready to let him go just yet.

"There was an accident on the mini-golf course, too," I said. "An antler came off that big fake moose."

"Really? Wow, didn't hear about that one. Were any employees hurt?"

"No, no employees were nearby." I didn't bother to tell him that *I* was the one the antler had almost landed on. Unless he was a better actor than I thought, I was pretty sure this was the first he was hearing about the incident.

"Crazy." He rubbed his chin. "Guess being friends with the assistant cruise director gets you all the gossip, huh? But listen, you can tell your friend Becca that John Sanchez wasn't involved in any of that stuff. He's a good kid." He glanced over his shoulder again. "Now if you'll excuse me . . ."

"Sure." I watched as he hurried back into the meeting room. I wasn't ready to take Fred's word that the busboy couldn't be our culprit. He had too much to gain by insisting that Sanchez had been wrongly terminated.

As for Fred himself? Now that I knew why he was

really on the ship, his suspicious behavior didn't seem so suspicious anymore. I was pretty sure I could cross him off the suspect list.

"Now this is traveling in style!" George exclaimed, settling back against her comfortable seat. "Where else can you sit on your rear end and get views like this?"

"No argument there," I said. "But you're going to give me a shot at the window seat sometime, right?"

George grinned. "Maybe. If you're nice to me."

We were aboard the train that was carrying us from Anchorage to Denali National Park. It was definitely a different experience from the train ride in Skagway. This train was a sleek, modern double-decker. We were on the top level, which featured two double rows of seats and enormous windows that offered an uninterrupted panoramic view of the scenery we were passing. The bottom level held the dining cars.

Alan leaned over from his seat beside Bess across the aisle. "Aren't you glad I talked you into coming, Nancy?" he whispered. "You wouldn't have wanted to miss this just to stay on the boat and keep an eye on you-know-who."

I glanced around to make sure nobody was listening. Luckily, all the nearby passengers were glued to their windows and paying no attention to our conversation.

"Yeah, you were right, Alan," I said. "I'm glad we're all here."

It was true. As it turned out, all my suspects except Max were going to be on the land tour. Well, and Fred—he'd stayed behind on the ship too. But when I'd told the others about my encounter with him, they'd agreed with my decision to cross him off the list. Becca had said she'd keep an eye on Max while we were gone, so I'd decided it wasn't worth leaving someone behind, especially for such a weak suspect.

Thinking about that reminded me that we'd been on the train for at least an hour, and I hadn't done a thing except admire the scenery. "Think I'll stretch my legs for a bit," I said, standing up.

"Good plan," George said, snapping a photo as the train rumbled over a bridge crossing a scenic river. "We've still got a long way to go."

I nodded. The trip to Denali would take about eight hours. That should give me plenty of time to check out all the suspects onboard. I'd already seen that Wendy and Hiro were in our car, and I figured Scott and Tatjana couldn't be too far away—most of the *Arctic Star* people seemed to be seated in the same section of the train.

Heading up the aisle, I came to Wendy first. Good. The blogger still wasn't my favorite suspect, and I was hoping I could cross her off my list with a few key questions. I mean, sure, maybe writing about odd happenings on the cruise could drive more viewers to her blog. At least, it had seemed like a decent motive when we were only talking about falling moose antlers and similar incidents. But it just didn't seem like a good enough reason to aid and abet a jewelry store robbery.

"Hey," I said, pausing beside her seat. "Enjoying the scenery?"

"Sure. What's not to like?" Wendy grinned up at me and patted the empty seat beside her. "Want to hang for a bit? Tobias's dad is sitting here, but he just left to take Tobias for a walk to see the rest of the train. Guess the kid was getting restless."

"Thanks." I sat down and glanced across the aisle, where Tobias's mother was staring out the window with her camera in hand. "So you're sitting with Tobias and his family, huh?"

"Yeah, we were talking last night at dinner, and they invited me to hang with them today," she replied. "They had an extra seat, and I didn't want to get stuck with some stranger." She barked out a laugh. "Anyway, they're cool, even if Tobias is kind of a pain. He's been freaking out about Hazel."

"The spider?" I couldn't help a slight shudder.

"Uh-huh. Their room steward is taking care of the thing back on the ship while they're gone, and Tobias is afraid she'll get squashed or something." She grinned. "Maybe Hazel should've tagged along. She could have had my seat. Now *that* would be a photo worth posting on my blog!"

I smiled. "Speaking of your blog, I bet all your readers will love reading about your adventures in Denali."

"Yeah, I hope so." A shadow passed across Wendy's face. "They're not exactly flocking to read about the trip so far."

"Really?" Apparently things hadn't picked up since I'd last talked to her, a couple of days earlier.

"Uh-huh." She picked at the back of the seat in front of her. "I was really hoping that blogging this trip would grab me some attention out there. You know— get some buzz going, maybe attract some advertisers or get me some paying gigs, whatever. Make this writing thing happen, you know?"

"Actually, I don't know that much about how blogs work," I said. "Do you mean you're hoping someone will want to pay you to turn your blog into a book or magazine article or something?"

"That would work." She cracked a rueful smile. "But really, I was just hoping maybe one of my posts might go viral. If it's big enough, something like that can lead to TV interviews or whatever, and then from there, who knows?"

"Oh." I wasn't sure what to think. It sounded as

if Wendy was doing everything she could to succeed at this blogging thing. Would that include helping a thief?

"Yeah, so here I am in this supercool place—" She sighed and glanced out the window. "And I still can't get anybody to pay attention. I'm starting to think this trip was a big, fat, expensive mistake."

"My friends and I won the cruise in a contest," I said. "I guess I didn't really think about how much it must cost."

"Let's put it this way," Wendy said. "My cousin works for one of the big travel websites and got me a serious discount. And I *still* had to sell my car to pay for it."

"Ouch." So much for crossing Wendy off the list. In my experience, desperate people sometimes did desperate things. And based on what she was saying, Wendy was as desperate as they came.

"Wah, wah, let me play the world's tiniest violin, right?" Then she wiggled her shoulders, as if shaking off her gloomy thoughts. "What will be will be, as they say. Anyway, look at me, spilling my guts to someone I just met, like, a week ago!" She laughed. "Sorry about that."

"It's okay," I said. "I understand how money troubles can get you down."

"Yeah. But when you get right down to it, I'm lucky I get the chance to, like, follow my bliss. That's enough reason to stay optimistic, right?" She grinned. "And hey, the trip's not over yet. Who knows, maybe somebody'll get eaten by a grizzly bear and I'll be there to document it!"

I noticed Tobias and his father making their way down the aisle. "Looks like your seatmate's back," I told Wendy. "I should go."

"Okay. But hey, thanks for listening."

"Anytime." I got up, exchanging greetings with Tobias and his father as I passed them.

Then I wandered up toward Hiro's seat. I'd been just about ready to cross Wendy off the suspect list, but this changed everything. Was it time to move her to the top?

Hiro was deep in conversation with another passenger. Not wanting to interrupt, I kept moving past his seat, planning to check the next car for Tatjana and Scott.

Before I reached the door, Alan caught up with me. "Hey," he said. "Glad I caught you. We heard we're about to pass through an area where you can sometimes see moose grazing in a field right along the train tracks! Come check it out."

"Oh. Um . . ." That did sound cool. But I wasn't really in the mood for wildlife watching.

But I should have known better than to protest. Alan wouldn't take no for an answer. Before I knew it, I was heading back toward our seats.

When I got there, I saw that George had moved across the aisle to sit with Bess. "What are you doing over there?" I asked.

George shrugged. "Bess had better snacks," she said. "Anyway, this is your chance to snag that window seat for a while."

"Good point." I glanced at Alan. "You don't mind, do you?"

"Go for it." He waved a hand toward the seats.

I sat down by the window, and he took the seat

beside me. For the next few minutes we watched for moose, but there was no sign of them.

"So where are the meese?" George asked, sounding impatient.

"Guess they're not out today," Alan said.

"Don't worry," Bess put in. "Even if we don't see any now, everyone says we'll see tons of them on our tour through Denali tomorrow. The wildlife viewing is supposed to be spectacular there."

"Cool." George grinned. "Think I'll get to pet one?"

"I don't think that's such a good idea," Bess said. "Moose actually injure more people in Alaska every year than grizzly bears."

"Really?" George sounded skeptical. "Where'd you hear that?"

"It's one of the fun facts in the brochure about this land tour," Bess said. "Didn't you read it?"

After a bit more bickering, the cousins went back to peering out their window, while Alan and I did the same. The two of us chitchatted about the scenery we were passing. But soon I was feeling restless again. The clock was ticking, and I didn't want to miss my chance to check out our suspects while we were all trapped on the train together.

"Excuse me," I said. "Think I'll go explore the train a little."

"No way, you can't leave now," Alan said with a grin. "We might still spot those moose!"

"No, seriously." I lowered my voice. "I want to go have a look around, if you know what I mean."

His eyes widened. "Oh!" he exclaimed. "Wait—do you have a new lead or something? Did one of the suspects do something suspicious?"

He was whispering, sort of. But his voice still seemed way too loud. "Shh," I cautioned, hoping the people in the seats nearby weren't paying attention.

"Oops. Sorry." He pressed a couple of fingers to his mouth, pretending to lock his lips shut. "But seriously," he whispered. "If you need help . . ."

"No, it's okay." I sighed and leaned back in my seat. "Actually, it can probably wait."

We still hadn't seen any moose—and I hadn't done any more investigating—by the time Hiro stood up and said it was time for our section of the car to head downstairs for lunch. George hopped to her feet immediately.

"Finally!" she exclaimed. "I'm starved!"

"Really?" Bess raised one perfectly groomed eyebrow. "Even after eating all my pretzels *and* my granola bar?"

George ignored that and stepped into the aisle. "Come on, let's get down there."

Alan stood and moved into the aisle behind her. "After you, ladies," he said, sweeping a hand forward in a little mock bow.

Bess smiled. "So gallant!" she cooed.

I crawled out of my seat and straightened up. "Thanks," I told Alan. As he leaned down to grab his knapsack off the floor beneath the seat, I caught up with Bess and George. When we started down the stairs, we saw Tobias and his family ahead of us. The little boy turned and spotted us.

"Hey, where's Alan?" he demanded.

"Right behind us." Bess glanced over her shoulder. "At least I thought he was."

"Here I am," Alan exclaimed, bursting into the stairwell. "Hey, Tobias. What's up? How's my girl Hazel?"

Bess, George, and I traded a glance as Alan and Tobias started chattering away, mostly about Tobias's pet spider. "I guess they must have bonded at the climbing wall yesterday," Bess murmured with a smile.

We all continued downstairs together. There were plenty of windows in the dining car, so we were able to enjoy more scenic views as we ate. Tobias was at the next table, along with his parents and Wendy. The little boy kept turning around in his seat to talk to Alan.

"What can I say?" Alan said with a grin. "I have a way with kids."

Tobias's mother heard him and turned with a smile. "Sorry if he's being a pest," she said. "He was so excited when he found out you were an environmental studies major. He wants to be a zookeeper when he grows up."

After the meal, we all headed back upstairs. Tobias went past his seat, following Alan down the aisle. "So do you get to study tarantulas in your college classes?" he asked.

"Dude, we study *every* kind of spider," Alan said with a laugh. "It's awesome!"

I glanced around the car to see if Hiro was free. He was nowhere in sight, so I decided maybe it was time to look for Scott and Tatjana. Bess and George had already taken their seats together, but I hovered beside my row, realizing I couldn't tell them what I was really doing. Not with Tobias hanging around and several other passengers close enough to hear.

"I'll be back in a bit," I said, patting my purse. "I'm going to the restroom to brush my teeth."

"Are you kidding?" Alan exclaimed. "Didn't you hear what our waiter told us just now? He said we'll be coming up on a great view of Mount McKinley soon. You don't want to miss that!"

His voice was loud and enthusiastic, as usual. I cringed as several nearby passengers turned to stare at us. So far, letting Alan in on our real purpose hadn't helped much with the undercover stuff.

"Um, okay," I said, figuring I could whisper my real plans to him once we sat down. "Want the window seat this time?"

"Nah, you can have it. I'm taller—I can see past you just fine." Alan stood back to let me by.

Stepping past him, I dropped into my seat. "Ow!" I cried as I felt something jab into my skin. I leaped up again, almost hitting my head on the curved glass of the window.

"What's wrong, Nancy?" Bess exclaimed.

I stared down in horror. "Glass! Shards of broken glass all over my seat!"

CHAPTER SEVEN

Narrowing the Field

"GLASS?" BESS CRIED. "WHAT DO YOU MEAN?"

I was bending down, examining the gleaming shards on my seat. They were silver, almost invisible against the upholstery. But they were definitely there.

Alan leaned closer. "Glass?" he exclaimed. "Are you sure?"

"Yes, I'm sure." I rubbed my backside. "Trust me."

The commotion from our seats was attracting attention. Tobias was still hanging around, and he pushed past Alan to peer at me.

"Hey, did the glass poke you in the *behind*?" he asked loudly.

I ignored him, carefully cleaning up the seat. Meanwhile Wendy appeared by our seats as well.

"Nancy?" she said. "What's going on? I heard you yell."

She sounded a little too eager. I glanced up and saw a camera in her hand. Could she have done this? Maybe set up a situation she thought could win her that breakthrough blog post she wanted?

"Someone dropped smashed glass on Nancy's seat," Bess told Wendy.

"What? You're kidding, right?" Wendy asked.

"I don't know." I forced a laugh. "But don't worry, everyone. I think I'll recover."

"Let me see those." Alan grabbed my hand for a closer look at the shards. "It looks like a glass was smashed—maybe from the dining car."

I squeezed my eyes shut. This situation was spinning out of control. The last thing I needed was to become some kind of mini-celebrity on this train. If everyone was watching me, it would be that much harder to do any investigating.

When I opened my eyes, Hiro was making his way toward us. "What's going on back here?" he asked.

"Nothing. I'm fine," I assured him.

"Nothing," Alan said quickly. "Except that someone put slivers of glass all over Nancy's seat. Anyone who would do that must be a sick person. Who knows what he or she might do?"

Hiro looked confused and concerned. "Okay, somebody had better fill me in here."

When he heard the story, Hiro insisted on contacting the train's security team. Several officers arrived moments later, shooing everyone in our car back down to the dining car while they searched the entire upper level. Finally we got the all clear and returned to our seats.

"Thanks for taking that glass for me, Nancy," George said, clearly trying to lighten the mood. "That was technically my seat, you know."

"I know. And you're welcome." I stuck out my tongue at her. "You want it back?"

"No way," Alan spoke up. "Go ahead and sit down, Nancy. After what you've just been through, you deserve the window seat. I'll sit right here with you and keep an eye out for any more trouble."

"Um, thanks." I sat down.

Across the aisle, I could see Bess and George with their heads bent close together, talking in whispers. I wished I could be over there with them, discussing this latest twist in the case. Because it had to be related, didn't it? There was no way it was a coincidence that broken glass had turned up on my seat.

A moment later my phone buzzed. I pulled it out and found a text from George.

BESS & I THINK U SHOULD GET CHECKED OUT BY A MEDIC WHEN WE GET TO DENALI, JUST IN CASE.

I didn't bother to text back; I just leaned forward so I could see past Alan to their seat. Both Bess and George were staring back at me. I rolled my eyes and shook my head.

A moment later, another text came:

SRSLY, NANCY. WHAT IF A. IS RIGHT AND SOMEONE

PUT SOMETHING ON THE SHARDS? COULD BE THE SAME PERSON WHO PUSHED U OFF THE WALKWAY IN K.

This time I typed a return text: LIKE U SAID, G, THE GLASS WASN'T ON MY SEAT. IT WAS ON YOURS.

George texted back again: HM, GOOD POINT. MAYBE THE BAD GUY IS AFTER ALL OF US NOW.

I realized I hadn't thought of that. Just then Alan glanced over.

"Who are you texting?" His voice sounded impossibly loud.

"Um, nobody," I said. "I mean, I'm just sending a note to Ned. My boyfriend."

"Oh, right." Alan nodded. "I met him that time we all went out to dinner together, remember? Nice dude."

I smiled weakly until he turned his attention back to the scenery. Then my fingers flew over the tiny keyboard. WHY WOULD SOMEONE BE AFTER U GUYS NOW?

The response came quickly: MAYBE WE R GETTING TOO CLOSE TO THE TRUTH.

I leaned back, feeling troubled. Could my friends be right? Were we all in danger now?

After a moment I texted them again: SO WHAT SHOULD WE DO?

The response: U SHOULD STAY PUT. B & I ARE GOING TO INVESTIGATE.

I frowned and texted: NO! IF SOMEONE IS AFTER U TOO, IT'S TOO DANGEROUS. WE NEED TO COME UP W/A PLAN.

I sent the text and waited for the response. Instead I heard the sounds of activity across the aisle. Glancing over, I saw Bess and George getting up.

"Where are you two going?" Alan asked before I could.

"Just taking a walk," Bess said sweetly. "Keep an eye on Nancy while we're gone, okay? She needs to relax and recover."

"Absolutely." Alan reached up and squeezed her arm as she went past.

"Hey!" I called as my friends hurried up the aisle. But neither of them responded. "Let me out," I told Alan. "I'm going with them."

"Ah, ah, ah!" He shook a playful finger in my face.

"You heard the lady. Relax and recover time."

I gritted my teeth, tempted to kick him in the kneecap and make my escape. But I held myself back. He was only trying to help. Besides, how much trouble could my friends get into on this train? I decided to let them go. Maybe I could convince Alan to lower his voice enough for the two of us to discuss the case. A fresh perspective might be just what I needed.

"Okay," I said, turning to glance out the window. "If anything can help me relax, it's looking at all this."

"I know, right? Beautiful."

We spent the next few minutes chatting about the scenery we were passing. At some point I realized it was probably the first time I'd ever had a real conversation with him, just the two of us. It was kind of weird. But kind of nice, too.

After a while Tobias appeared. Seeing my friends' empty seats across from us, he flopped into the aisle seat. "Hey, Alan," he said. "My dad says Mount McKinley is the tallest mountain on the whole continent. Is that true?"

Alan grinned at him. "Hey there, little man," he said. "I bet your dad is right."

"Oh." Tobias looked impressed. "Do you study mountains and stuff in your classes, or just animals?"

"We study it all," Alan replied. "The whole shebang."

I looked at him. For a while, I'd almost forgotten that he wasn't on this trip only because of Bess. He was also supposed to be getting a head start on his college research project for the next year.

"That reminds me," I said. "Have you had any ideas for your big sophomore project yet?"

"Not really," he said. "But it'll come. I'm just taking it all in, letting it simmer."

"Need any help brainstorming?" I offered. "I'm usually pretty good at coming up with ideas for stuff like that. What are the parameters of the project?"

Tobias sat up and perched on the edge of the seat. "Do you have to write a report for school?" he asked Alan. "You should write about spiders! I got an A on the report I did about Hazel."

"Cool," Alan told him. Then he glanced at me.

"And thanks. Maybe sometime, I guess."

"Wait! I have a better idea." Tobias swung his leg around, kicking the seat in front of him. "You could write about the bone smugglers!"

"The what?" Alan asked.

"My mom read about it in the newspaper when we were getting ready for this trip." The kid sounded excited. "She said the police arrested some guy for stealing tusks and bones and stuff from rare Alaskan animals." He poked Alan on the arm. "Which Alaskan animals are the rarest? Think we'll see any when we tour the park tomorrow?"

"I don't know, little buddy. What do you mean by rare?" Alan said.

"He probably means endangered species," I put in. I wasn't too interested in their conversation, though I couldn't help being a little surprised that Alan didn't seem to know much about Alaskan wildlife. Still, I guessed an environmental studies degree covered a lot of ground. He couldn't be expected to know everything about every eco-system in the world, especially after only a year of study.

"Right." Alan shrugged. "Maybe you can ask the tour guide at Denali about it, Tobias." He grinned. "You can also ask him if there are any tarantulas there!"

I shot him a look, pretty sure he had to be kidding this time. Even I was pretty sure that tarantulas were mostly found in warmer parts of the world.

"Yeah, right," I said. "Tarantulas in Alaska?"

"Hey, there are spiders everywhere, right?" Alan shrugged again. Then his face lit up. "Here come Bess and George."

I glanced up and saw my friends hurrying toward us. Tobias saw them too and jumped out of their seats.

"Switch places back?" Alan said, standing up quickly as they reached us. "No offense, Nancy. But I miss my best girl."

"Sure, whatevs." George flopped down beside me. "Yo."

"Yo yourself. Find out anything interesting?" I asked quietly.

She took a quick look around. Tobias was hanging on the back of Alan's seat across the way, still chattering away at him about grizzly bear skulls or something.

"We tracked down Scott and chatted with him for a while," George told me. "We realized there's no way he's our guy."

"Really? How come?"

"Because he was in full view of a number of people up on the main deck from the time we arrived to the time you found that note in your luggage." She added, "In the detective biz, we call that lack of opportunity."

"Thanks for the lesson, detective." I rolled my eyes. "But I see your point. And I guess his weird behavior on the train could be explained away by the gambling stuff he told me about when I saw him meeting with those tough guys in Ketchikan. If he's still in debt, he's probably stressed, especially if that sort of thing could get him fired if anyone finds out." I thought back to that scary encounter. "No wonder he wasn't thrilled to catch me listening in on his phone conversation, even by accident, since he knows I know about his problem."

George nodded. "Next we went looking for Tatjana.

We found her, but didn't get to talk to her much. She blew us off after, like, three minutes. Said something about needing to go downstairs to take care of some paperwork."

"Hmm. Think she was telling the truth?"

"Who knows? Everything she says sounds mysterious in that crazy Russian-sounding accent of hers. But that's probably because I've watched too many old *Rocky and Bullwinkle* cartoons." George grinned. "Anyway, we looked for Hiro on our way back here, but we couldn't find him."

"No mystery there. He's probably still with the security people or something." I was still thinking about Tatjana. She'd been on the list for a while, but we hadn't really investigated her very much. "Anyway, we can talk to him later. For now, I'm thinking maybe we should focus on finding out more about Tatjana."

"Wow, that was a long train ride." George stretched as we all climbed off the bus that had carried us from the train to the lodge where we would be staying that night, a pleasantly rustic place on the outskirts of Denali National Park. "I can't believe it's only four in the afternoon."

"Yeah, well, we left Anchorage pretty early," I pointed out.

"After all that sitting, I'm ready to go out and stretch my legs," Alan put in, slinging Bess's carry-on bag over his shoulder. "Good thing I booked us on that horseback-riding excursion this afternoon. It should be a nice long ride, since it stays light so late here this time of year. Come on, we'd better get checked in and changed or we'll be late."

I traded a look with my friends. As usual, Alan had signed us all up for an activity without checking in first. Not that I had anything against horseback riding. But I'd been hoping to have some free time to investigate this afternoon, since from what Scott had told us, we'd be on our Denali bus tour for most of the following day.

As we entered the lodge's impressive wood-and-stone lobby, I noticed Tatjana standing off to one side of the check-in desk. She was chatting with the ABCs and a couple of other passengers. Okay, maybe this was my chance.

"Can you guys check us in?" I asked Bess and George. "I just want to, um, look around the lobby."

Bess followed my gaze and nodded. "Of course."

"Thanks." As they headed for the check-in desk, I eased closer to Tatjana. The other passengers were talking excitedly about the scenery they'd seen that day. As Babs described her impressions of a particularly scenic gulch, I hovered on the edge of the group, waiting for an opportunity to join the conversation.

Before I got the chance, I was distracted by the sound of George's voice. Her very *loud* voice.

"What are you talking about?" she exclaimed. "What do you mean, our reservation was canceled?"

CHAPTER EIGHT

Reservations

THE NEXT FEW MINUTES WERE PRETTY chaotic. I rushed over to find the lodge staff apologizing profusely, saying that someone had called the day before to cancel the reservation for the cabin Bess, George, and I were supposed to be sharing. The interesting thing? Nobody seemed to know exactly who the caller had been. He or she—nobody seemed sure about that, either—hadn't left a name.

Soon Tatjana and Hiro appeared and got involved, and they were still trying to work things out when the buses arrived to take people off to the various afternoon excursions, including the horseback ride Alan had booked for the four of us. Deciding to look for the silver lining in the situation, I offered to stay behind and straighten out the room mix-up while my friends went on the excursion. Maybe I would have my chance to investigate today after all.

Alan still didn't seem to catch on to the whole silver-lining angle, since he tried to change my mind, insisting that Tatjana and Hiro could take care of it for us. Luckily, Bess and George were a little more savvy. They dragged him off toward their bus.

The lobby cleared out quickly as most of my fellow passengers headed off on their activities. Within minutes the place was all but deserted, though I noticed Wendy paging through some brochures over near the entrance. It looked as if she'd decided to skip today's optional trips. No wonder, after what she'd told me earlier. Becca had arranged for Superstar to comp all the activities my friends and I did, but I'd caught a glimpse of the prices when Scott had passed out some information earlier. Most of the activities weren't exactly cheap, especially for someone in Wendy's financial situation.

Thinking of Scott reminded me of what my friends had figured out. Thinking back, it *did* seem unlikely that he could have planted that threatening note. Unless he'd had help from someone else—like Max, for instance. This whole time we'd been focusing on *one* person who could be the jewelry thief's accomplice. What if there was more than one person involved? If so, maybe we shouldn't be so quick to cross someone like Scott off the list. True, he probably couldn't have left me that note. And it seemed unlikely he could have been the one to push me off that Ketchikan walkway, either, since I'd seen him heading in the opposite direction shortly beforehand. But what about the other stuff—the moose antler, the loud argument I'd overheard in the ship's kitchen, the pre-cruise problems, and of course sneaking the robber aboard? There was no reason he couldn't have been involved in any of those incidents.

It was an interesting thought. But Scott had disappeared, presumably to accompany the excursion groups, so I turned my attention to two handier suspects, Hiro and Tatjana. They were still having a stern discussion with the front desk staff. I stepped back and watched the pair. What if one of them had canceled that reservation? It certainly would have been easy for either of them to do it. But why? Was it just another way to throw me off balance, warn me not to mess with them?

I looked around for Wendy again, but she'd disappeared. There were only a few other passengers still lingering in the lobby. An elderly couple sitting by the fireplace. A cluster of women heading into the dining room. A woman with an active young toddler from the redheaded reunion group.

I watched as the redheaded mother led her child around by one chubby hand. The redheads had been around when I'd been pushed off that walkway. And the whole extended family seemed kind of excitable. What if one of them had bumped me by accident? That would mean the whole Ketchikan incident was a red herring—no pun intended.

But if one of the redheads had bumped me,

wouldn't he or she have noticed and fessed up? And wouldn't that person have been the one to call for help instead of Alan?

Thinking about the incident in Ketchikan brought my mind back around to Scott again—and the rough-looking guys he'd met with there. Okay, so he had a reasonable explanation for meeting them, and I had enough sleuthing experience to know I shouldn't jump to conclusions based on appearance. That didn't change the fact that both those guys would be totally believable as robbers or thugs in the movies. What if my new theory was right, and I needed to be looking for more than one culprit? What if Scott was one of them, and had helped one of his "poker buddies" onto the ship?

Pulling out my phone, I sent a quick text to Becca, asking for a description of the thief the police had arrested.

My phone rang almost immediately. It was Becca.

"Got your text," she said. "I don't know what the guy looks like, but I can try to find out."

"Cool, thanks," I said. "Anything interesting happening on the ship?"

"Not really," she replied. "But I've been asking around about John."

"John?" For a moment I couldn't place the name. "Oh! You mean the fired busboy?"

"Yeah." I heard her sigh. "The more I talk to people who know him, the weirder that whole situation seems. Everyone swears he's the nicest, most honest guy around. Nobody I've talked to can imagine him getting mixed up with drugs." She paused. "Do you think that could mean something? Is it connected to our case somehow?"

"I don't know. But I'll keep it in mind. Call or text as soon as you find out about the jewelry thief, okay?"

"Will do."

Wandering closer to the desk, I found that Tatjana and Hiro were still working arrangements out with the lodge staff. "Don't worry, Nancy," Hiro told me. "We'll have this sorted out shortly."

"Thanks," I said.

As I watched them, my mind returned to my new theory. If we really were looking for two culprits instead of one, which pairings made the most sense? I'd already thought of Scott and Max—Scott could have smuggled the robber aboard, Max could have planted the note, and either of them could have fiddled with the moose antler, though neither of them made sense as the walkway pusher. Besides, what connection did they have to each other? Did some other pairing make more sense? Maybe Max and Hiro, or Scott and Tatjana?

I was about to text Becca again to see if she knew of any connections among our suspects. But at that moment I spotted Wendy wandering toward me.

"Hey, Nancy," she said. "Why aren't you off white-water rafting or whatever?"

I quickly explained the room situation, watching her closely for any sign that she already knew about it. But she barely seemed to pay attention. In fact, she seemed distracted and a little jittery.

"Bummer," she said. "But listen, epic news. I was

just hanging outside chatting with some peeps and surfing the net, and I think I came up with a fab new idea to promote the blog!"

"That's great," I said. "What is it?"

She grinned, tapping her laptop, which was tucked under one arm as usual. "Top secret for now," she said with a coy smile. "You'll have to wait and see after my investigation is complete!"

With that, she hurried off, humming under her breath. I stared after her, feeling troubled. What kind of "investigation" was she talking about?

I started to follow her, but Tatjana intercepted me. "Good news, Nancy," she said. "I can show you to your room now. The porters are already fetching your luggage."

"Thanks." I followed her out of the main lodge building. Most of the guest rooms were located in small separate cabins out back.

Tatjana led me to a cabin at the edge of the complex. It overlooked a small meadow dotted with wildflowers. Beyond that began a thick tangle of forest.

"Very nice, yes?" Tatjana said as we stepped inside. "They gave you an upgrade due to the misunderstanding."

The place *was* very nice. There was a small sitting room, a full bath, and three bedrooms. Our luggage was already piled near the door.

"It looks great," I said. "Thanks for straightening this out."

I glanced at her, trying to figure out a way to question her about the case. But she was already on her way out the door. "Have a lovely evening, Miss Drew," she called over her shoulder.

"You too," I said, though she was already gone.

With a shrug, I walked over to the coffee table and dropped my purse on it. I could unpack later. Right now I wanted to get back out there.

First, though, I headed into the bathroom to wash my hands. As I reached for the towel hanging under the window, I caught a glimpse of movement outside.

I took a better look, guessing it might be some of

the area's well-known wildlife. Instead I saw Tatjana tiptoeing past, heading for the woods!

"What?" I murmured, all my detective instincts suddenly on alert.

Dropping the towel, I raced outside and around to the back of the cabin. By the time I got there, Tatjana was just disappearing into the woods.

I sprinted across the meadow, hoping she didn't look back—and also hoping that nobody else was looking out the windows of the nearby cabins. Luckily, Tatjana didn't seem to realize she was being followed. As I ducked into the shade of the thick evergreens, I could hear her footsteps up ahead, crunching on the dried pine needles that carpeted the forest floor.

My heart pounded as I followed, trying to keep a little quieter myself. Was I about to solve the case?

I trailed her for about five minutes. Finally she stopped short in a pretty little sun-dappled clearing. Huddling behind a broad tree trunk at the edge, I watched as she glanced around, then pulled a compact out of her pocket and applied a fresh coat of lipstick. Weird. What was she doing out here?

I was so focused on watching Tatjana that it took me a moment to notice the hurried footsteps coming up behind me. By the time I tuned in, it was too late. I spun around.

"Hey!" Hiro blurted out, looking as startled as I was. "What are you doing here?"

CHAPTER NINE

Strange Discoveries

"HIRO!" MY HEART POUNDED AS I RECOGNIZED the danger I was in. We were pretty far from the lodge out here—definitely too far for anyone to hear me scream if Tatjana and Hiro were up to no good.

I glanced back at Tatjana, who was coming toward us. "Nancy!" she cried, her eyes flashing with anger. "Did you follow me?"

"Obviously she did," Hiro snapped, frowning at her. "I told you to be careful!"

I cringed back against the tree trunk as he spun to face me. My eyes darted around, looking for anything I could grab to use as a weapon—a rock, a fallen branch . . .

"Nancy, please don't tell anyone you saw us out here," Hiro begged.

I blinked, focusing back on his face. All the anger had disappeared from his expression. Now he just looked anxious and kind of freaked-out.

"Yes, please, Nancy," Tatjana put in. "If anyone knows we are together, especially Becca—"

"Wait," I said, confused. "What's going on here?"

Hiro reached for Tatjana's hand. "Don't worry," he told her, his voice thick with emotion. "Even if they fire us, it was worth it." He planted a kiss on her lips.

I blinked. Okay, I'm no Bess, but I recognize romance when I see it. "So you two are—a couple?" I asked. "That's why you're sneaking around out here?"

"Yes." Tatjana squared her shoulders. "But you cannot tell Becca. She wouldn't understand."

Hiro nodded. "I know you're friendly with Becca," he told me. "So I suppose you already know that she and I used to date when we both worked for Jubilee."

"Actually, I didn't know that." But now that I did, some things were starting to make a lot more sense.

"We broke up when we both got hired by Superstar." He shrugged. "She's technically my boss now, so we didn't think it would be appropriate to keep seeing each other. Then Tatjana came along. . . ." He glanced over at Tatjana and squeezed her hand, which he was still clutching. "Anyway, we weren't sure at first how serious things were between us, so we kept our relationship a secret."

Tatjana added, "It seemed a good idea at the time."

"Yes. But now that things are more serious, we're worried that Becca won't understand." Hiro sighed, running his free hand through his spiky dark hair. "In fact, I'd planned to talk to her about it before now, but I can't seem to catch her alone."

"That's why you burst in on us," I realized. "At the snack bar the other day. You were looking for Becca, right?"

He nodded. "I ran into Omar—the kid who works at that snack bar—and he said she was up there." He smiled ruefully. "I didn't even stop to think that she might not be alone."

"Sorry about that." My mind was clicking along, adding this piece to my puzzle of clues and incidents. This explained why Becca and Hiro always seemed so awkward together. And why Becca never had much to say when I questioned her about him. And also why Tatjana had been harder for her to reach lately.

"You won't tell her, will you?" Hiro asked anxiously.

"I plan to talk to her as soon as we get back to the ship."

"I won't say a word."

Leaving them together, I headed back through the woods toward the lodge. Halfway there another thought occurred to me. Could this new information also explain the busboy's firing? Maybe he'd caught the two of them together, and they'd been afraid he'd tell Becca. . . .

"Doubtful," I muttered before I'd even finished the thought. It was worth keeping the possibility in the back of my mind, but now that I knew their secret, Hiro and Tatjana just didn't seem like the type of people who could have made that anonymous tip against an innocent man.

When I reached the meadow, I saw a flash of movement. It was Tobias. He was crouched near the edge of the woods with a digital camera.

I walked over to him. "What are you doing out here?" I asked. "I thought you'd be off on a day trip."

"Nope." Tobias straightened up. "My mom had a headache, so we stayed here." He grinned. "Good thing, too! Wendy wants me to take pictures of all the birds and animals and stuff I can find. She says she'll pay me if she decides to use any of them on her website!"

"Really? Are you sure she said that?"

"Uh-huh." Tobias turned and snapped a photo of a bird flying past. "She knows I like exotic animals and stuff, so she figures I can get some good ones."

"And she said she'd pay you for them?" That seemed odd, given that Wendy was supposed to be broke. Could this have something to do with her mysterious new plan?

Tobias stared at me as if I had two heads. "Didn't I just *say* that?"

"Where is Wendy right now?" I asked.

Tobias shrugged, fiddling with his camera. "She was in the lobby when I saw her."

I headed for the lobby, but Wendy wasn't there. She wasn't in her room or the restaurant, either. I wandered around the grounds for a while, but there was still no sign of her.

"Oh well," I murmured, pausing on the lodge's unoccupied back deck.

The lounge chairs out there looked comfortable, so I sank onto one. It had been another long day. I leaned back, staring up at the still-bright early evening sky and thinking about the case. I realized I'd just crossed two more suspects off my list. The more I thought about it, the more certain I was that Hiro and Tatjana didn't have anything to do with the case. That only left me with a few live suspects: Wendy, Max, maybe Scott. Was it time to start looking for some new ideas?

Pulling out my phone, I checked to see if Becca

had texted back yet about my questions. She hadn't, and I was about to stick the phone back in my pocket when I realized I hadn't checked in with Ned in a couple of days.

I tapped out a quick message to him, mostly saying hi and updating him on the case. It was pretty late in River Heights due to the time difference, so I wasn't expecting an answer until the next day.

Hearing a noise, I looked up and saw Tobias creeping along in the distance near the woods. He was too far away for me to see whatever bird or other local critter he was focused on, but seeing him reminded me of what he'd just told me.

Why would Wendy pay him for photos? It had to have something to do with her new plan. But what kind of money-making scheme could involve amateur photos of Alaskan animals? I wondered if Alan might have any guesses. After all, he was the expert on wildlife and such.

At least he was *supposed* to be. Suddenly I remembered the odd answers he'd given Tobias on the train earlier. It had almost sounded as if he didn't know much about the native creatures of Alaska. But wouldn't an environmental studies major know about things like that, especially if he was planning to make this trip the basis of a yearlong school project?

That brought another question to mind. What if Alan wasn't what he claimed to be? I sat up straight, disturbed by the idea. But I couldn't quite shake it. After all, Bess had just met Alan a few weeks ago—she really didn't know him that well yet. Could he be pulling some kind of scam on her or something?

"You're letting this mystery go to your head, Drew," I said to myself with a half smile. I glanced down at the message on my phone screen, hesitating for only a moment before adding a few quick lines, asking Ned to check up on Alan when he got the chance. That shouldn't be hard, since they were both students at the university.

I hit send and leaned back in the lounge chair again. There. With that taken care of, I could go back to working on the case—beginning with tracking down Wendy. Still, the lounge chair was comfortable, and the evening temperature was perfect. Maybe I could just sit here and rest for a few minutes first. . . .

My eyes drifted shut, and moments later I was asleep.

Unfortunately, my unplanned siesta made it hard to fall asleep that night. It didn't help that it never really seemed to get dark in Alaska at that time of year. When Bess, George, and Alan returned from their ride at almost nine o'clock, it was still as bright as midday. And when we all headed into our separate rooms a couple of hours later, the sun was just sinking toward the horizon. I tossed and turned and finally drifted off after a while, but awoke suddenly at around two a.m.

Yawning widely, I got up and tiptoed toward the bathroom, trying to be quiet so I wouldn't wake Bess and George. After using the facilities, I wandered over to the sink to wash my hands. I glanced out the window at the moonlit landscape.

I blinked. Was the near darkness playing tricks on my eyes? Or was that a hooded figure sneaking off toward the woods?

My sleepy mind struggled to figure out what this meant. I pressed my nose to the window, trying to get a better look. Was that Hiro sneaking off to meet Tatjana?

I blinked again, trying to focus my fuzzy mind. Maybe it was Hiro, or Tatjana for that matter. But what if it wasn't?

That thought woke me up a little more. Hurrying out to the main room, I slipped on the shoes I'd left near the door and pulled a jacket over the shorts and tee I was sleeping in. Then I let myself out of the cabin as quietly as I could.

The figure had disappeared by the time I rounded the cabin and crossed the meadow. But he or she had been heading toward the same trail into the woods that Tatjana had used earlier, so I hurried that way too.

The woods were a lot darker and spookier at this time of night. Animal calls and rustling noises came from every direction. I did my best to ignore them, listening for any sound of human footsteps.

Enough moonlight filtered through the treetops for me to follow the narrow trail through the woods.

I hurried along until the trail split, then hesitated. Tatjana had gone right earlier. Should I go that way now?

Then I heard the crack of a branch somewhere off to the left. I turned and went that way.

After walking for a few more minutes, I started to doubt my decision. I hadn't heard another sound from up ahead. What if that cracking branch had been caused by an animal? My quarry could be a long way down the other fork by now.

Then I froze as I heard a sudden loud sound up ahead. It was muffled by the trees surrounding me, and I wasn't sure what had caused it. It didn't sound like footsteps—more like a loud but muffled grunt or squeal. What if it was an animal?

My heart pounded as I suddenly flashed back to all those wildlife warnings they'd given us on this cruise. Not to mention Bess's comments about dangerous moose, and Tobias's excited talk about grizzly bears and other native wildlife. What if I was about to stumble across a bear, a wolf, an irritated moose?

I stayed rooted in place, waiting for the sound to come again. But all I heard were the normal noises of the forest. Finally I crept forward again, moving slowly and carefully, wondering if I was being foolish. Maybe it would be smarter to go back to the lodge, get some backup. . . .

Then I saw the trees open up into a clearing just ahead. It was larger than the one where Hiro and Tatjana had met earlier. But that wasn't the only difference. This clearing had a ramshackle corrugated shed in the middle of it.

I crouched behind a tree and scanned the clearing for the hooded figure. When nothing moved, I stepped carefully into the clearing.

The shed's door was standing ajar. I realized that could explain what I'd heard—a rusty metal door scraping over the earth might make just that sort of weird sound. Scurrying over, I peered inside. It was dark in there, of course, and at first I couldn't see a thing.

Then my eyes adjusted a little, and I saw something large and square shoved into the darkest corner. A box?

What was it doing way out here? And what was inside?

I carefully dragged it out. It was fairly large and surprisingly heavy. When I peeled back the packing tape holding it shut, a strange musty odor tickled my nose, and I let out a sneeze.

BANG!

Suddenly a shot rang out. I gasped and jumped back as a bullet pinged off the metal shed wall—inches from my head!

CHAPTER TEN

New Connections

ACTING ON INSTINCT, I LUNGED FOR COVER behind the shed as another gunshot exploded out of the woods. Leaping across the clearing and into the trees, I ran for my life.

My breath came in ragged gasps, making it hard to hear whether anyone was following me. But no more shots came. Finally I dared to slow to a jog and glanced up at the moon, trying to gauge which direction I needed to go to return to the lodge. I made my best guess and circled around that way, hoping I wasn't too far off. If I went the wrong way, I could end up hopelessly lost in countless acres of Alaskan wilderness.

It wasn't a comforting thought. I ran as fast as I dared, trying not to make too much noise. After a while I found myself on a trail. Was it the same one I'd taken in? I had no idea. The trees all looked the same, and I couldn't see the moon anymore through the thick canopy overhead.

Just as I was starting to fear I'd gone the wrong way, that I was racing ever deeper into the forest, I caught a glimmer of light through the trees ahead. Could it be the lodge? I ran faster, glancing back over my shoulder for pursuers. . . .

CRASH!

I let out a shrill scream as I smashed into something. Make that some*one*. "Nancy?" a familiar voice said.

Glancing up, I blinked in surprise. "S-scott," I stammered.

Panic grabbed me for a second. Was Scott the person I'd followed? Had that light come from the flashlight he was using to track me? Was he about to finish the job he'd started back in the clearing?

Then I blinked as I realized we were standing at the edge of the woods. The lodge was right there on the other side of the meadow, and there was a light on in one of the cabins—that was the glimmer I'd seen through the trees. Scott wasn't holding a flashlight. He wasn't wearing a dark hoodie, either—just jeans and a T-shirt.

I slumped with relief, gulping in deep breaths of air to try to catch my breath. "Sorry I crashed into you," I said as soon as I could talk again.

"It's okay." Scott looked concerned. "What are you doing out here this time of night? I saw you wandering into the woods a little while ago."

"Y-you did?" I glanced at those nearby cabins. Several had windows facing onto this meadow, just like mine. More lights were blinking on in some of them now. Obviously my scream had awakened people. Oops.

Scott nodded. "I got dressed and came out to see if I could catch up to you," he said. "I was afraid you might not realize how dangerous the Alaskan wilderness can be, especially at night."

"Yeah, no kidding." I took a deep breath, looking

back at the dark forest. "Um, did you hear gunshots a few minutes ago?"

"Gunshots? Come to think of it, I guess I did. Probably some locals hunting or something. Why? Is that what scared you?"

I hesitated, not sure whether to trust him with what had really happened. By then I could see several people hurrying across the meadow toward us. In the lead was a big, beefy guy in a security guard's uniform.

"What's going on out here?" he asked in a deep voice.

I glanced at his name tag, which identified him as Hank. "Sorry," I said with an apologetic smile. "I couldn't sleep, so I went for a walk."

Bess and George arrived moments later. George was rubbing her eyes, looking less than half awake, but Bess pushed her way forward. "Nancy, are you okay?" she exclaimed. "We heard a scream, then realized you were gone. What happened?"

"I went walking in the woods and stumbled across a shed out in a clearing." I waved a hand in the general direction of the forest. "There was a box inside, and I was about to open it to see what was inside when someone shot at me."

Gasps came from all around. "Shot at you?" Hank the security guard said. "Are you sure?"

"Absolutely. The bullet landed close enough for me to see it."

Hank looked grim. "I'd better go out and have a look around," he said, patting the holster at his waist.

"I'll come with you," Scott offered. "I want to know what's going on out there."

A couple of other men also volunteered to go along. Soon the group was tramping off into the woods, following my vague directions to the clearing.

"Come on, Nancy." Bess put an arm around my shoulders. "Let's get you inside."

We went into the main building, where one of the hotel's night staff rustled up some hot tea. Some of the other people I'd awakened were there too, so I couldn't tell Bess and George the rest of the story, though they kept giving me curious looks. Half an hour later, the men finally returned.

I jumped to my feet and hurried over. "Well?" I asked Hank.

"We found your shed," he said. "But there was no box there. And no sign of the shooter." He shrugged. "Did see a coupla fresh bullet holes in the wall, though."

"The box was gone?" My heart sank, though I supposed I shouldn't be surprised. Instead of chasing me, the shooter must have grabbed the box.

"We'll notify the police just in case," Hank said. "But chances are it was a hunter who mistook you for a hare or something."

"Okay," I said. "But that doesn't explain the box."

"Hmm." Hank didn't quite meet my eye. "Maybe it was a cooler of beer or something."

"It definitely wasn't any kind of cooler," I insisted. "It was a cardboard box, about this big." I made a shape with my hands. "It smelled really weird, like whatever was inside had been stored in a moldy basement or something."

"Well, I'll let the cops know about that. Now you'd better get to bed, miss."

I frowned, annoyed, as I realized he didn't care about the box or what may have been in it. Why would I make up something like that?

Still, it wasn't as if I could prove anything. So I let it go. Maybe my friends and I could hike back out there in the morning and look around.

"I still can't believe someone actually shot at you last night," Bess said as she slathered butter on a piece of toast.

"You're not the only one." I glanced around the lodge's homey restaurant. It was early, but lots of people from our group were there having breakfast. Scott was among them; he was sitting at a large table with the ABCs and a couple of people I didn't know. As I scanned the room, I caught several people watching me. Was one of them the hooded figure I'd followed into the woods? It was a creepy thought.

George noticed the glances too. "You're the talk of the lodge, Nancy," she commented. "Everyone's buzzing about what happened last night."

"Yeah. I can't believe nobody woke me up." Alan speared a sausage with his fork. "I missed the whole thing."

"It's okay, sweetie." Bess patted his hand. "Nancy's fine, and that's what matters."

The other tables were too close to risk talking about the case, so we spent the next few minutes chatting about the day's plans while we ate. We were scheduled to catch a bus over to the visitor center of Denali National Park in a couple of hours. There, we would split up into several smaller buses for an all-day guided tour.

Finally Bess took one last sip of her grapefruit juice. "I'm stuffed," she said. "Think I'll take a walk. Want to come?" She smiled at Alan.

He jumped up, dabbing some syrup off his face with a napkin. "Sounds good."

"Have fun," George said, reaching for another slice of bacon.

As Bess and Alan made their way out of the crowded restaurant, Wendy hurried in past them. She glanced around, then made a beeline for our table.

"Uh-oh," I told George under my breath. "Bet I'm about to be interviewed for the next big blog post."

George smirked, but didn't have time to say anything before Wendy reached us. "Nancy!" the blogger exclaimed breathlessly. "I heard you were in here. Everyone's all atwitter about you, you know. What really happened last night, anyway? I tried to talk to that security guard afterward, but the dude wouldn't tell me a thing."

"There wasn't much to tell," I said. "I just wandered into the woods, and I guess someone out there wasn't happy to see me."

"Oh." To my surprise, Wendy didn't seem too interested. Shooting a look around, she set her laptop on the table and sank into the seat Bess had just vacated. "But listen, I just figured out who you really are."

I blinked. "Um, what?"

"You're the big-time amateur detective from the Midwest, right? Don't tell me there's another Nancy Drew out there who looks just like you."

I exchanged a slightly panicky look with George. "Uh . . ."

"Don't worry. If you're here, like, investigating a case or something, I won't blow your cover." Wendy waved a hand. "But this totally changes things. I might be willing to share my thing—*if* you promise to give me the scoop for my blog, that is."

"Your thing?" I echoed.

"Wait," George broke in. "How'd you figure out that Nancy's a detective?"

Wendy shrugged and reached for piece of bacon. "It wasn't that hard." She popped the bacon into her mouth, continuing to talk as she chewed. "I've noticed how Nancy always seems to be around when weird things happen. So when I found out about the mysterious stuff going on around here, I wondered if . . . Well, you know."

Her smile looked a little sheepish. I realized what that meant. *I'd* been one of *her* suspects!

"So anyway, I did a little research after all the excitement last night. Made me miss some beauty sleep, but I didn't want to wait." She grimaced. "I heard there's not much in the way of wireless access once we're out in the park. We might not even have cell phone coverage."

"Go figure," George said innocently.

"Yeah." Wendy shrugged. "Anyway, it didn't take me long to find tons of info on you, Nancy."

"Really?" I said. "Like what?"

Wendy opened her laptop and slid it over in front of me. "Here you go."

My eyes widened. She'd opened up some kind of search engine. There on the screen was a whole page's worth of stories about me! There were articles from the River Heights paper about various cases I'd solved. A write-up of a local service award I'd received last year. Even a link to a video of me standing beside my father while he was interviewed on TV after winning a big case.

"Wow," I said. "I mean, I know you can find just about everything online. But this is kind of creepy!"

George reached for her coffee cup. "I'm always telling you this stuff is out there, Nancy." She glanced at Wendy and rolled her eyes. "I swear, sometimes you'd think Nancy was older than my grandma."

I just stared at the screen. This whole time, I'd been wondering why someone would target me and my friends when we were supposed to be here undercover. But when you came right down to it, we weren't really undercover at all. We were using our real names. Anyone with Internet access could find out who we were with the click of a mouse.

The realization was so overwhelming that it took me a moment to realize Wendy was still talking. "Anyway," she was saying, "I figured it made sense for us to team up to solve the case, you know?"

"The case?" I gulped. "Um, how did you find out about it?"

Wendy shrugged. "The news is out there—all you have to do is look for it," she said. "But actually, it was Tobias who clued me in."

"Tobias?" I shot a confused look at George, who shook her head. "Wait, how did Tobias know about it?"

"I don't know. I guess he saw it online too," Wendy said. "The kid's really into weird animal stuff, in case you haven't noticed."

"Weird animal stuff?" George said. "Wait—what case are you talking about?"

"Duh—*my* case." Wendy sounded a little impatient. "And yours too, maybe, I guess. Are you here to investigate the Alaskan smuggling ring?"

"Smuggling ring?" I echoed. "Um, no. What smuggling ring?"

"Seriously? That's not why you're here?" Wendy looked suspicious. Then she shrugged. "Look, I'll show you."

She grabbed the laptop and started typing. A moment later she shoved it over to me again.

Another search result was up on the screen. This time, all the links had to do with smuggling. Specifically, smuggling animal parts, like tusks, teeth, and bones of rare or endangered species.

"Wow," I said. "Check this out, George."

We skimmed a few of the articles, many of which talked about the latest international smuggling ring, which the authorities had so far been unable to bust. I felt a growing sense of excitement as I read. Was this the puzzle piece I'd been looking for?

"Well, here's a motive for us," George said, clearly

thinking the same thing. "What if someone's been smuggling rare Alaskan animal parts into Vancouver on cruise ships? It says right here that Vancouver's a big hub for that sort of thing."

"Wait," Wendy broke in. "You think whoever's doing this is someone from our ship? Crazy!"

"Maybe. And this would explain the weird, musty smell coming from that box last night." I couldn't help shuddering at the thought that the box might have been full of animal bones and such. "The trouble is, how do we prove it? We don't know who that figure in the hoodie was. And we don't even have the box as evidence."

Just then I noticed a security guard hurrying toward us. He was a different guy from the one last night.

"Nancy Drew?" he said. "Hi. Hank filled me in on your situation during shift change this morning. I just wanted to let you know that the local police are on the case. We'll keep you posted. In the meantime, just holler if you need anything. My name's John." He pointed to his name tag.

"Thanks, John." I stared at his name tag, and suddenly the final puzzle piece clicked into place in my head. A grin spread over my face. "Thank you very, very much!"

"What are you looking so happy about all of a sudden?" George asked as the guard hurried away.

"I think I know how to find out who I followed into the woods last night," I said. "Maybe even how to solve the entire case—*if* it's not too late."

"Really?" Wendy exclaimed. "How can I help?"

"Can you go online and find out someone's cell phone number?" I asked. "Even if it's a super-common name—like Fred Smith?"

CHAPTER ELEVEN

Final Surprise

"AMAZING, NANCY," GEORGE SAID. "I CAN'T believe you figured things out just from some security guy's name tag."

We were sitting in the lobby of the lodge with Bess, Alan, and Wendy. The police were still there. They were dragging Scott toward the door, though he wasn't going easily. He was sputtering with anger and calling the cops every name in the book. It was getting close to time for the buses to leave for the park, and a lot of our fellow *Arctic Star* passengers were in the lobby, watching the show.

"Well, *I* can't believe Scott was our culprit all along," Bess said. "I figured he was off the hook, since we knew he couldn't have planted that note in Nancy's bag."

"I still don't understand exactly what happened," Alan complained. "Anyone care to fill me in?"

"Scott was the hooded person I followed into the woods last night," I told him. "He was going to meet his contact at that shed. He needed to confirm that the contact had brought the box of illegal stuff—and probably also needed to pay him for it, of course. Then Scott could smuggle the box onto the *Arctic Star* and pass it off to someone else when he got back to Vancouver."

"So was Scott the one who shot at you?" George asked.

"I don't think so," I replied. "That was the contact. It seems Scott had already left the shed area by the time I got there. See, he was planning to leave the box in the shed until we were all off touring Denali today. Then he'd have plenty of time to go get it and hide it somewhere." I shrugged. "He was already back at the lodge—and had removed that hoodie—by the time he heard the shots. He was doubling back to see what was going on when I stumbled into him."

"Then what happened to the box?" Alan wondered.

"Like I said, Scott's contact took those shots at me. I guess he heard me crashing around in the woods and hid to see what was going on." I grimaced. "Once he scared me off, he must've moved the box to a different hiding place, which is why the security guard didn't see it. But the police found it when they searched Scott's room just now."

"Wow." Bess shook her head. "Wait—but you still haven't told us how you figured out it was Scott."

"That's where Fred Smith came in." I traded a smile with Wendy. "See, the security guard who came to update me this morning was named John. That reminded me that I've been hearing that name a lot lately."

"So?" Alan looked confused. "John's a pretty common name."

I smiled. "Right. That's why it took so long for me to put two and two together. John Sanchez is the name of the busboy who got fired—and framed, according to

Fred Smith." I shrugged. "John is also the name of one of the people I overheard arguing in the kitchen our first night on the ship."

"I almost forgot about that," George said. "I always figured that was just a red herring, since it seemed so random."

"Yeah, I wasn't too sure myself," I said. "But I realized that the John from that argument could've been John the busboy. And that maybe someone was threatening him because he'd stumbled on to something incriminating."

Bess's eyes widened. "I get it!" she exclaimed. "Everyone says John the busboy is super honest, right? He found out about what Scott was doing, so Scott framed him to get him fired."

"Not at first," I said. "I guess Scott thought his threats were enough to keep John quiet for a while. But when Vince and Lacey got arrested and security was tightened—and especially after the jewelry store got robbed—he decided it was safer to just get him out of the picture."

"So Scott was involved in the jewelry store thing, too?" Wendy asked.

"Uh-huh. The police already got him to fess us to that. He loaned his ship ID to one of his sleazy friends—probably one of the guys I saw him meeting with in Ketchikan. The guy was only supposed to pick up something from Scott's cabin, but on his way out I guess he decided the jewelry store looked like easy pickings."

"Wow," George said. "But wait. I still don't get how you knew Scott was behind all this."

"I didn't," I admitted. "Like I was saying, that's where Fred Smith came in. He was trying to help John the busboy, so I figured he was our best bet to get John to tell us who threatened him in the kitchen that day."

"Scott?" Alan guessed.

I nodded. "Scott was the one who framed him. He also threatened his friends and family, so John was too scared to go to the police even after he got fired. But Fred talked him into telling him the truth."

"Cool." Wendy looked impressed. "So the case is

closed." She leaned over and poked me. "Don't forget, you promised I could break the news on my blog. Exclusive interview, right?"

I hesitated. I wasn't thrilled about having this story splashed all over Wendy's travel blog, especially after seeing all the information about me out there on the Internet already. Still, Wendy had provided a key clue in solving the case. Maybe I owed her that scoop.

"Um, sure," I said uncertainly. "But can we do it later? It looks like the bus is here." I pointed to the large bus pulling to a stop outside.

George jumped to her feet. "Come on, let's go get in line."

We were waiting to board the bus when Tatjana found us. "I just finished talking with the police," she told me. "I thought you'd like to know that Scott is agreeing to make a full confession about the smuggling business." She pursed her lips and shook her head disapprovingly. "I still can't believe he's a criminal!"

"But he confessed to everything?" I asked.

She shrugged. "Almost everything. He realized he'd

get off easier if he ratted out the rest of the smuggling ring. He also confessed to planting those drugs to get John Sanchez fired. And to giving that Troy Anderson fellow his security card to get him on the ship." She smirked. "He was pretty angry that the guy robbed the jewelry store on his way out, since he blames that for getting him busted."

"He didn't know that Nancy was on the case." George clapped me on the back. "She always gets her man!"

"Hmm." Tatjana didn't look too impressed by that. "Anyway, it seems he was also responsible for some funny business Becca was worried about before the cruise. Probably to distract her from his real mission."

I nodded, thinking back over the various troubling little incidents Becca had told me about, checking those off my mental list. "What about the falling moose ant-ler, and the glass on my seat?" I asked. "Oh, and the note in my suitcase—we know he couldn't have done that himself, but if he got someone else to do it . . ."

I trailed off. Tatjana was shaking her head. "I don't know anything about any of that. Scott claims he had no idea you were investigating him. He had no reason to try to hurt you." She glanced at her watch. "Excuse me. I need to start getting things organized."

She hurried off. "Never mind, Nancy," Bess said. "I know you like to tie up all the loose ends, but those things are no big deal."

"She's right," George added. "We knew all along that the fallen moose could've been an accident."

"On my seat? By the window?" That didn't seem super likely to me. "And what about the note in my suitcase?"

George glanced over at Tobias, who was waiting with his parents a few yards away. "Maybe that was a prank," she said, nodding toward him. "You-know-who's cabin is right next to ours, and we all know he's a bit, uh, exuberant."

There was no more time to discuss it as Tatjana, Hiro, and the bus driver starting herding us all onto the bus. I realized there were a few other loose ends we hadn't discussed—like my fall into the creek in Ketchikan, our canceled reservation, even the crazy laundry mix-up. I couldn't help wondering if there was yet another culprit still out there—maybe Max? But no, he probably couldn't have pushed me off that walkway, and he definitely couldn't have planted the glass. . . .

My phone buzzed, interrupting my thoughts. It was Becca texting me with a description of the jewelry thief. "Too bad I didn't think to ask that question earlier," I murmured as I scanned the message.

"Huh?" George glanced over at me. She'd snagged the window seat yet again.

"I asked Becca to find out what the jewelry thief looks like," I said, showing her the text. "She just heard back from the cops, who described him as an average-size white male in his mid-thirties with a large scar bisecting his face. Just like one of the guys I saw with Scott in Ketchikan."

"Whoa. If we'd known that earlier . . . ," George began.

I nodded, staring at the phone's little screen. "I know."

Hiro was walking up the aisle, checking names off a list. He paused by our seats and grinned. "Better get all your calls and texts in now," he said, gesturing toward my phone. "Won't be much cell coverage out in the park."

"So I've heard." I smiled back, then tucked my phone away. "But that's okay. I'm sure we'll have better things to do than chat on the phone."

As the bus pulled away from the lodge, I did my best to shake off those last few doubts. Maybe my friends were right. We'd solved two separate cases already. What were a few minor loose ends, anyway?

It wasn't too hard to put the case out of my mind as we entered Denali National Park. Three smaller buses were lined up, waiting for us. They looked like school buses that had been painted green. Tatjana had already divided our group into three, and we all headed for our assigned buses. My friends and I ended up on the first to depart.

As we trundled off down the road, I glanced around at my fellow passengers. The ABCs and a few other acquaintances from the ship were onboard, along with Tatjana. However, Hiro, Wendy, Tobias and his family, and others were on the other two buses.

Within minutes, the visitor center had disappeared

behind us, and we were surrounded by wilderness as far as the eye could see. A great greenish-yellow plain stretched out on either side of the road, and we almost immediately spotted a herd of caribou grazing in the distance. Farther off were gorgeous snowcapped mountains, including Mount McKinley, which our guide, a chipper young woman, told us most Alaskans referred to by its original native name, Denali. She also told us that the park covered around six million acres, and that the road we were on was the only one in the entire place.

We were kept busy for the next couple of hours admiring the scenery and spotting wildlife. The bus stopped a few times so we could get out and take pictures—of Dall sheep high up on a cliff, a family of grizzly bears in the valley below the road, and a particularly scenic overpass.

The bus had paused to let a moose cross the road when my phone rang. George was taking pictures through the front windscreen, but she looked over at me in surprise. "Hey, you still have a signal! Who is it?" she asked.

"Don't know." I checked the readout. "Oh, it's Ned! Wonder why he's calling instead of texting?"

Bess smiled. "Duh. He probably misses hearing your voice."

I stuck out my tongue at her as I picked up the call. "Ned!" I exclaimed. "I miss you. How are you? What time is it there?"

"Nancy?" His voice sounded fuzzy and very far away. Glancing at the readout, I saw that I barely had one bar's worth of reception.

"Ned? I can hardly hear you. I'm in the middle of Denali National Park, and—"

"Nancy, listen," he cut me off. "I checked into this Alan guy like you asked, and I—"

BZZZ. The line went dead.

"Ned?" I said.

"Dropped?" George asked.

"Yeah. No surprise, I guess." I shrugged, not wanting to mention what he'd said, since Alan and Bess were in the seat right behind us. "Guess I'll call him back when we get back to the lodge."

I couldn't help wondering what Ned had found out about Alan. Was it good news or bad news?

George was still taking pictures of the moose, which seemed to be taking its time ambling across the road. "Good thing Tobias isn't on our bus," she said. "He'd probably want to get out and say hello."

"Be nice," Bess said, leaning forward from her seat. "That kid knows a lot about animals. He probably knows moose can be dangerous."

I glanced back to see if the other buses had caught up to ours yet. But there was no sign of them. "Looks like Mr. Moose is moving on," I said. "He might be gone before Tobias's bus gets here."

The tour continued. Our guide used the moose's appearance to warn us once more about keeping a safe distance from the animals, especially the larger and more dangerous ones. Alan raised his hand.

"My girlfriend claims moose are more dangerous than grizzly bears," he said with a grin. "True or false?"

"Depends how you look at it," the guide responded. "It's true that people have been hurt and killed by both species. Moose aren't normally as aggressive as bears, though females with young can be quite protective. But due to their numbers and large size . . ."

I barely heard the rest of the guide's answer, distracted by wondering once again about Alan. Was he just joking around by asking a question like that? Or was it a clue that he might not be what he seemed? I wished Ned had been able to finish whatever he was trying to tell me.

But there was no point in fretting about it now. Even if Ned had found out something bad—like that Alan was only posing as a university student to impress Bess—there wasn't much I could do about it at the moment. If there was another mystery there, it could wait until we got home to River Heights.

Oohs and aahs were rising around me, and I realized we'd just come into view of a gorgeous lake. I didn't waste another thought on anything but soaking up the scenery until we stopped at a picnic grounds for lunch.

The lunch spot was just as scenic as the rest of the park. It overlooked part of the valley, with rocky foothills behind it. We all ate quickly, talking about everything we'd seen so far. Then people scattered in different directions, snapping photos of scenery, wildflowers, and some Dall sheep visible on a ridge nearby. I pulled out my own camera to get a shot of a curious ptarmigan, but as the bird waddled away, I once again found myself feeling a little distracted. I just couldn't seem to totally forget about those loose ends—especially that note in my suitcase and the smashed glass on my seat. It was hard to believe either of those things was an accident or even a prank. But who could have done them? And why?

I wandered off by myself around a pile of boulders, not wanting Bess and George to notice my expression. They both know me pretty well, and I wasn't in the mood for their teasing. Leaning against one of the rocks, I stared at the mountains in the distance and tried to puzzle out some answers.

"Nancy!" Alan burst into view, breathless and giddy. "You have to come check this out. I just spotted a litter of adorable baby foxes!"

"Really?" The guide had mentioned that we would

probably encounter some foxes in the park, though we hadn't seen any yet. "Where are they? Did you tell Bess and George?"

He tugged on my sleeve. "Hurry, before they wander off," he urged. "I'll find Bess and George and bring them over."

I tried to shake off my distraction. "Okay. Where are they?"

He pointed to an outcropping nearby. "That way. Just climb over those rocks and down the other side and you'll see them."

"Cool." As he rushed off in the other direction, I headed for the outcropping. I was still deep in thought as I carefully picked my way over the rocky ground and clambered down the steep far side. That put me in a little valley near a creek sheltered on three sides by rocky slopes.

I glanced around, but there were no foxes in sight. Hearing a noise behind me, I turned around—and found myself face-to-face with an irritated-looking moose and her calf!

CHAPTER TWELVE

Final Answers at Last

"OH!" I BLURTED OUT BEFORE I COULD STOP myself. My mind raced; what had that guide told us about mother moose being dangerously protective of their babies? I wished I'd paid more attention. "Easy does it."

The moose lowered her head, her ears back and her hackles raised. She grunted, moving her huge body between me and the calf.

I glanced over my shoulder, ready to scramble back up the slope. But it was steep and pretty high. Would I have time to make it to safety before the moose charged?

Or was it better to stand still and hope she'd realize I wasn't a threat? Those seemed to be my only two choices, since the moose were blocking any other escape.

Then I heard footsteps at the top of the rocky slope. Glancing up, I saw Alan peering down at me.

"Thank goodness!" I cried. "Alan, quick—toss a stone or something behind the moose to distract it, then help me up!"

Alan bent and picked up a rock. He wound up and threw it—right at the baby moose!

The calf bleated in surprise and pain as the rock bounced off its head. That riled up the mother moose even more. She took a step toward me.

"What are you doing?" I cried. "I said throw it *behind* them, not *at* them!"

Alan smirked. "I was hoping for a grizzly bear," he said. "But thanks to Encyclopedia Bess, I figured Mama Moose here would do just as well."

I gaped up at him, my brain not quite processing what he was saying. But he wasn't quite finished.

"Maybe this will teach your father not to meddle

in other people's lives," he growled, throwing another stone at the baby moose.

Luckily, that one missed. But the mother moose was pawing now, looking really angry. Alan picked up a large rock, tossing it from hand to hand.

"D-don't do this, Alan," I said, my voice shaky. "Bess and George will be along soon."

"Don't count on it," Alan sneered. "I just sent them off looking for those imaginary fox kits—in the other direction."

Despite the danger, my mind couldn't help fitting this piece into the puzzle. "It was *you*!" I said as realization dawned. "You're the one who was responsible for all those loose ends!"

"Ding-ding-ding! Give that lady a prize," he said sarcastically. "Took you long enough to figure it out." He hefted the rock. "You know—for such a fabulous detective."

I gulped, glancing at the moose. If Alan threw one more rock at her baby, I was pretty sure it would be the last straw. I had to distract him.

"So you were the one who left that note in my suit-case?" I asked, trying to keep my voice from shaking.

"That was an easy one," he said with a mirthless laugh. "I pretended I'd left my passport in my suitcase. Nobody even gave me a second look when I was paw-ing through our bags. I switched the tags on your suit-case and slipped that note inside."

He actually sounded proud of himself. "Okay, good one," I said, pressing back against the rock wall and trying to keep my voice calm. The moose eyed me sus-piciously and let out a snort, but stayed where she was. "Um, so what about the mini-golf moose thing? Was that you too?"

"Of course. I was just bummed that the antler mostly missed you." Alan looked at the real moose, seeming amused. "Who knew it was the real version that would finish you off?"

"And you pushed me off the walkway in Ketchikan, didn't you?" Now that I thought back, I couldn't believe I hadn't seen it sooner. "I could have been killed!"

"Bingo!" His mouth twisted with amusement. "Not

that it wasn't fun to mess with you in smaller ways too. Like changing your wake-up call, and bumping George so she'd knock your bagel on the floor, and getting all your clean laundry sent out. Oh, and canceling your reservations yesterday too."

"And the glass all over my seat?" I waited for the answer, though I already knew it.

"That too." Alan sounded impatient. "But enough chitchat. I know you're stalling. Or are you just trying to get me to confess?" He barked out a laugh as he hoisted the rock again. "Because if that's your game, you might as well give it up. You can't prove anything, even if Mama Moose doesn't trample you."

"She won't have to," a confident but rather high-pitched voice rang out behind him. "We just heard you confess to everything!"

Alan dropped his rock and spun around in surprise. Tobias stepped into view, with Wendy right behind him.

"The kid's right," Wendy said. "We heard it all."

Tobias glared at Alan. "I came to look for you when our bus got here," he said. "I wanted to ask you if there were any interesting spiders around this place."

Alan didn't respond. Casting a desperate look around, he shoved past Wendy and took off running. "Guys?" I called up as gently as I could, keeping one eye on the mother moose. "A little help here?"

"Right." Tobias grabbed the rock Alan had dropped. He hurled it a few yards behind the moose, where it landed in some weeds with a thud.

The mother moose heard it and spun around, shoving her calf aside and snorting suspiciously at the spot where the rock had landed.

Meanwhile Wendy bent and stretched a hand down, then grabbed my arm and helped to pull me up as I scrambled for safety. Whew!

"Where'd he go?" I asked as soon as I caught my breath. "Hurry—we have to find him! Who knows what he's capable of?"

"I still can't believe Alan was after you this whole time," Bess said. "How stupid am I?"

I glanced at her. She and George and I were on the

lodge's back deck, relaxing in lounge chairs and enjoying the bright Alaska evening.

"Don't beat yourself up," I said. "He had us all fooled."

"Not me," George put in with a frown. "I never liked the jerk."

"You never like any of the guys Bess dates," I reminded her with a half smile.

The smile faded as I sighed, thinking back on the events of the day. Everything was kind of a blur for the few minutes after I'd climbed out of that moose pit. Wendy, Tobias, and I ran back and told Hiro and Tatjana what had happened. A search was mounted, and Alan was found quickly. There weren't many places to hide in the sparse landscape, and Alan wasn't much of an outdoorsman.

Soon the bus driver was radioing for help, and we were waiting for the police to come and take Alan away. In the meantime, he'd had quite a bit to say. Apparently my father had been the prosecuting attorney who'd helped get Alan's father put away for life for fraud and embezzlement. Alan had vowed revenge, but he'd decided that just going after my dad wasn't enough. He wanted to hurt him by hurting his family—which meant me. And that must have been what Ned was calling to tell me before the call was dropped.

That was the whole reason he'd pursued Bess. He'd figured it would be an easy way to get close to me, figure out my weaknesses. The Alaska trip was a lucky break for him. It had given him lots of opportunities to mess with me.

Then he'd found out that I really was a pretty accomplished sleuth. That had made him realize he needed to up the ante. He'd started watching for a chance to *really* hurt me. His original plan had involved causing an accident during that horseback excursion I'd ended up skipping, but spotting that mother moose had provided him with a second chance.

"I couldn't believe the way he kept threatening you, even when the police were dragging him away." Bess shivered, wrapping her arms around herself. "Swearing he'd never rest until you and your dad paid . . . What a nut!"

"Good thing Wendy recorded his whole rant on her smartphone." George grinned. "I loved the way she waved the phone in his face and told him she was going to forward it to the police." She leaned back in her chair. "You know, I thought that chick was a real weirdo at first. But she's okay."

"Tobias, too," Bess put in. "I'm glad he finally started to enjoy this vacation. He's actually kind of a cool kid."

I glanced at her with a wry smile. "It just goes to show that people aren't always what they seem."

"No kidding," Bess said with feeling. "I still can't believe I fell for a jerk like Alan."

We heard the door swing open behind us. Sitting up, I saw Wendy hurrying over.

"There you are!" she said. "Listen, I know you've had a tough day, Nance. But I'd love to get a post about this whole dealio up before the story hits the wires." She winked. "Nothing like an exclusive for a little free publicity, right? So how about it? Can we do that interview now? Maybe get some photos of the day's hero?" She formed her hands into a mock camera lens, framing me inside it.

Once again, I hesitated. I *really* owed her now. But I still didn't like the thought of losing even more of my anonymity if she got her wish and the story went viral.

"I've got an even better idea," I told her. "You should focus your story on the *real* hero of today."

"Who, the moose?" George put in. "You're right, she showed great restraint in not stomping you. But I doubt she's in any mood for interviews."

I ignored her, standing up and smiling at Wendy. "Let's go find Tobias," I said. "I'm thinking maybe you could focus your story around him. Isn't that the kind of thing that's more likely to go viral? Kid hero saves the day?"

Wendy's eyebrows shot up. "Oh my gosh, you're so right!" she exclaimed. "I know I can get some serious attention with that story. Nancy, you're a total genius!"

"You don't know the half of it," George said with a smirk.

But Wendy was already heading for the lobby, shouting for us to hurry up and follow. "Come on," I told my friends with a smile. "Let's go help her track down her new victim—er, I mean star."

"And maybe *then* we'll be able to relax and enjoy the rest of the trip?" Bess said.

I grinned. "Definitely."

Dear Diary,

WOW! THAT'S ABOUT ALL I CAN SAY.

I would never have believed that the bones of endangered animals were valuable enough to be smuggled.

But almost more incredible was that Alan posed as Bess's boyfriend just to get revenge on me.

As spectacular as Alaska was—Mount McKinley did take my breath away—I can't wait to get back to River Heights.

'Cause in the end, there's no place like home.

READ WHAT HAPPENS IN THE NEXT MYSTERY

IN THE NANCY DREW DIARIES,

Mystery of the Midnight Rider

"IS THAT HER?" I ASKED, SHADING MY EYES against the glare of the afternoon sun. "The one in the beige breeches and tall boots?"

Ned grinned. "You'll have to be more specific, Nancy. Just about everyone out there is wearing beige breeches and tall boots."

The two of us were leaning on the rail of a large riding ring at the local fairgrounds. At the moment it was crowded with horses and riders warming up for their next class. All of them—male and female, teenagers and adults—were dressed almost exactly alike.

"You have a point," I said with a laugh. "So how are we supposed to know who to cheer for once the class starts?"

Just then one of the horses separated from the others and trotted toward us. "Ned Nickerson? Is that you?" the rider called.

Ned waved. "Hi, Payton! It's good to see you again."

"You too." Payton halted her horse in front of us and smiled shyly. She was about sixteen, with a slender build and delicate features that made her look tiny atop her horse, an enormous bay with a splash of white on its forehead.

"Payton, this is my girlfriend, Nancy Drew," Ned said. "Nancy, this is Payton Evans."

"Nice to meet you," I said. "Your horse is beautiful."

"Thanks." Payton leaned forward to give the horse a pat on its gleaming neck. "He's actually not mine, though. I'm riding him for my trainer—he's one of her sale horses. He's still a little green, but he's coming along."

"Green?" Ned raised an eyebrow. "Looks kind of reddish-brown to me."

I rolled my eyes at the lame joke. "Green just means he's not fully trained yet," I explained.

"That's right." Payton smiled at me. "Are you a rider, Nancy?"

"Not really." I shrugged. "But I took some lessons when I was a kid. And I never miss coming out to watch this show." I returned her smile. "Even when I'm *not* acquainted with one of the star riders."

I glanced around, taking in the hustle and bustle surrounding me. The annual River Heights Horse Show was a prestigious competition, attracting top hunter-jumper riders from all over the country.

Payton's smile faded slightly. "I'm not the star," she said, her voice so soft I could barely hear it over the thud of hoofbeats and chatter of riders and spectators. "The horses are the stars. I'm just along for the ride."

"You don't have to be modest," I told her with a chuckle. "Ned's told me all about you. He says you've been riding since you were practically in diapers, you've had all kinds of success on the A circuit, and that you're supertalented and hard working."

Payton shrugged, playing with the tiny braids in her mount's mane. When she responded her voice was even quieter. "It's easy to work hard at something you love."

As an experienced amateur detective, I'm pretty good at picking up clues. But it didn't take a super-sleuth to tell that Payton wasn't comfortable with our current line of conversation. Time for a change of subject.

"Anyway," I said, "Ned also tells me your mom and his mom were college roommates."

"That's right." Payton stroked her mount as he snorted at a leaf blowing past. "When Mrs. Nickerson heard I was coming to this show, she was nice enough to offer to let me stay with them so I don't have to stay in a hotel."

"She's thrilled to have you here, and she can't wait to see you tonight," Ned assured Payton. "I'm supposed to tell you not to eat too much today, since she and Dad are planning a big welcome barbecue for you tonight."

I chuckled. "That sounds like your parents," I told

Ned. "So are Payton's parents going to be staying with you too?"

"No," Payton answered before Ned could say anything. A sad look flitted across her face. "They have to stay in New York for work today and tomorrow, and then they've got a family obligation that will keep them busy for most of Saturday. But they promised they'll be here in time to watch me ride in the Grand Prix on Saturday."

"The Grand Prix? What's that?" Ned asked.

I rolled my eyes at him. "Weren't you paying attention when I dragged you to this show last year?" I joked. "The Grand Prix is the big jumping competition on Saturday night. It's sort of like the equestrian competitions you see in the Olympics. Huge, colorful fences that are, like, ten feet high."

Payton laughed. "Not quite," she said. "Even the best Olympic horse couldn't jump a ten-foot fence! The heights are more like five feet."

"Close enough," I said with a shrug. "Anything I can't step over myself looks high to me."

Ned poked me on the shoulder. "Here come Bess and George," he said. "I was wondering where they'd disappeared to."

"Bess said she wanted to grab a soda." I noticed that Payton looked slightly confused as she watched my two best friends approach. "George is short for Georgia," I explained with a wink. "But nobody calls her that unless they're trying to get under her skin."

Payton nodded. "Got it."

By then Bess and George had reached us. Both had sodas, and George was also holding a paper cup of French fries smothered in ketchup. The scent of grease wafted toward me, temporarily overwhelming the pleasant horsey smell of Payton's mount.

"Payton Evans, George Fayne, Bess Marvin," Ned said, pointing at each girl in turn as he made the introductions. "Bess and George are cousins, believe it or not," he added with a grin.

"What do you mean 'believe it or not'?" Payton asked.

I laughed. Bess and George may share the same

family, but that's about all they have in common. Bess is blond, blue-eyed, and as girly as they come. George is, well, pretty much the opposite of that. For instance, Bess had dressed up to come to today's show in a pretty dress, stylish flats, even a matching bow holding back her shoulder-length hair. George? She was wearing what she wore just about every day. Jeans, T-shirt, and sneakers.

"Don't pay any attention to him," Bess said. "It's nice to meet you, Payton."

"So you're the superstar rider Ned keeps talking about," George added, popping a fry into her mouth. "He's been totally geeking out about how you're probably going to be in the next Olympics. Is that true, or is he just pulling our legs?"

Payton shrugged, playing with the reins resting on her mount's withers. "Actually my trainer tells me the Chef d'Equipe of the US team is supposed to come watch the Grand Prix at this show."

"The chef de what?" Bess asked as she reached over and snagged one of George's fries.

"That's the person in charge of the Olympic team," Ned explained. "Mom and Dad were talking about it last night after Payton's dad called to make final arrangements."

"Wow," I said. "So this big-time Olympics guy is coming to watch you ride? Maybe so he can decide if you should try out for the US team?"

"I guess so." Payton shrugged again. "I mean, we don't know for sure that he's coming to see me in particular. But my trainer and my parents seem to think so."

"Awesome." George reached out and tentatively patted Payton's horse on the nose. "So is this the horse you'll be riding when he's watching?"

"No. I'll be riding my own horse—my most experienced jumper. His name is Midnight." Payton smiled as she said the horse's name. "He's really cool. Maybe you guys can meet him later."

"We'd love to," Bess said. "As long as it's not *too* much later. Because I'm sure Nancy and Ned have other plans this evening." She waggled her eyebrows at me.

"Sure we do," Ned said. "My parents are throwing that barbecue tonight, remember? You're both invited."

"Oh, right." Bess pursed her lips. "Okay, but that's not what I'm talking about." She waggled a playful finger in Ned's face. "I certainly hope you're planning to take Nancy somewhere more romantic than a family barbecue—or a horse show—this weekend. It's your anniversary, remember?"

"How could he forget? You've only been reminding him twice a day for the past month." I was exaggerating, but only a little. Bess is nothing if not a romantic.

"Yeah. Give it a rest already," George told her cousin. "I'm sure Ned has it all under control."

"Of course I do. I mean, what could be more romantic than this?" Ned slipped one arm around my shoulders, helping himself to a couple of George's fries with the other hand. "Fried food, horse manure—what more could any girl want?"

"Heads up!" a voice barked out, cutting through our laughter. It was another rider—a sharp-chinned teenage girl on a lanky gray horse. The horse was cantering straight at Payton and her mount!

Payton glanced over her shoulder, then shifted her horse aside just in time to avoid a collision. "Um, sorry," she called to the other rider, even though from where I stood it looked as if the gray horse was the one at fault.

The gray horse's rider pulled him to a halt and glared back over her shoulder. "Is this your first horse show, Payton?" she snapped. "This is supposed to be a warm-up ring. If you want to stand around and gossip, do it somewhere else."

"Sorry," Payton said again, though the other rider was already spurring her horse back into a canter.

"Nice girl," George commented with a snort. "Friend of yours?"

Payton sighed. "That's Jessica. I don't even know her that well—she rides at a barn a few miles from mine, and we end up at most of the same shows. I have no idea why she doesn't like me, but she's never exactly made a secret of it." She grimaced and gathered up her reins. "But she's right about one thing—I shouldn't be standing around. I'd better get back to my warm-up. I'll see you guys later, right?"

"Sure. Good luck," Bess said.

We watched her ride off. "She seems nice," I said to Ned.

"Yeah, she is." Ned reached for another fry despite George's grumbles. "Our moms try to get together as often as they can, so I've known Payton for a long time. Haven't seen her in two or three years though." He licked the salt off his fingers. "Her parents both have pretty intense jobs. Mr. Evans is some kind of high-powered financier, and Payton's mom is a medical researcher at one of the top hospitals in New York City."

"Wow." George whistled. "Impressive."

"Yeah. And I guess what they say is true—the apple doesn't fall far from the tree. Because Payton's kind of intense herself." Ned glanced out toward the ring. "Her parents say she started begging for riding lessons when she was about three or four, and she's spent every possible minute in the saddle since. I guess it's no wonder people are starting to talk about the Olympics."

Turning to follow his gaze, I saw Payton cantering the big bay horse near the center of the ring, where several jumps were set up. Her face was scrunched up with concentration as she steered around the other riders going every which way. As I watched, she aimed her mount at the highest of the jumps. I held my breath as the horse sailed over easily.

"Nice," Bess said.

"Yeah," I agreed. "I can't wait to see her compete. How long until it's her turn?"

"I'm not sure." Ned glanced at the gate a short distance away. A steady stream of riders had been going in and out the whole time we'd been standing there.

"I guess you'll have to follow the clues to figure it out, Nancy," George joked.

I grinned. My friends like to tease me about my recreational sleuthing. But the truth is, they seem to like it just as much as I do. At least, they never complain when I drag them into yet another case. Not much, anyway.

We all watched Payton and her horse glide easily over another jump. As she landed, I caught a flurry of activity immediately behind where my friends and I were standing. Glancing over my shoulder, I saw a woman striding in our direction. She was petite and deeply tanned with close-cropped reddish-blond hair a few shades darker than my own. As she rushed past us to the rail, the woman was so focused on the activity in the ring that she almost knocked Bess's soda out of her hand.

"Payton!" she hollered. Her voice was surprisingly loud for such a small person, cutting easily through the clamor of the warm-up ring. "Over here—now!"

Soon Payton was riding over again. "Dana!" she said breathlessly. "I thought you were going to meet me at the in-gate." She glanced at us. "So did you meet Ned and his friends? Guys, this is my trainer, Dana Kinney."

"Huh?" Dana barely spared us a glance and a curt nod. "Listen, Payton, we need to talk—now."

"What is it?" Payton checked her watch. "I was

about to leave for the ring. I'm on deck, I think."

"Then I'll make this quick." Dana clenched her fists at her sides, staring up at Payton. "One of the show stewards just received an anonymous tip about you."

"About me?" Payton looked confused. "What do you mean? What kind of tip?"

Dana scowled. "Whoever-it-is is claiming that you drug all of your horses!"

New mystery.
New suspense.
New danger.

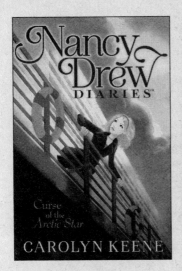

All-new Nancy Drew series!

BY CAROLYN KEENE

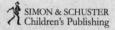